Sketches and S

Sketches and Secrets of Summer

A Pride and Prejudice Novel

LEENIE BROWN

LEENIE B BOOKS
HALIFAX

No part of this book may be reproduced in any form, except in the case of brief quotations embodied in critical articles or reviews, without written permission from its publisher and author.

This book is a work of fiction. All names, events, and places are a product of this author's imagination. If any name, event and/or place did exist, it is purely by coincidence that it appears in this book.

Cover design by Leenie B Books. Images sourced from Deposit Photos and Period Images.

Sketches and Secrets of Summer ©2021 Leenie Brown. All Rights Reserved, except where otherwise noted.

ISBN: (ebook) 978-1-989410-92-9; (paperback) 978-1-989410-93-6

Contents

Chapter 1

Derbyshire was beautiful in the summertime. It was perhaps the most beautiful spot in the world. At least, Stuart Alford had always thought so. Of course, the beauty of this county and his affinity for it had not stopped him from avoiding home for several years. Indeed, he would still be avoiding it if it were not for that horrible, black-edged letter that he had received six weeks ago from his younger brother.

Blasted death! Why must it strike everyone? And why must it, in its wake, thrust unwanted possessions on those whom it had not yet claimed? Was not the sorrow of separation enough?

Stuart had been downright content being a solicitor and man of business for his friend in Devon. He had been set up in a pretty, little cottage with a small staff. It was just the proper size for a bachelor such as himself. Life had been filled just full enough with activity and friends to provide entertainment and companionship, and there had been enough undulation to the landscape to keep it from being boring. There was also the added benefit of being able to see some craggy rock faces if he wished for a reminder of home. It only required that he take a drive to the coast.

Ah! The ocean. If there was anything in particular that was lacking in Derbyshire, it was that there was no ocean. There were lakes that were filled with great stores of water, but not even the largest of them could compete with the majesty of the ocean. Not unexpectedly, he had not fully understood that fact until he had visited his friend's home between school terms one year and had been captivated by the great expanse of water that stretched from the shore to the horizon and beyond.

How long would it be before he would be able to look upon the grandeur of the sea once again? His heart sighed. It was entirely possible, and most likely probable, that it would never happen again. There was a staggering volume of work to be done at Wellworth Abbey. His brother had only recently undertaken a refreshment project for the house. Rooms were in disarray. Tradesmen were waiting for payment and instructions. There were also the books that needed to be reconciled for this month, and then? He blew out a great breath.

And then, there were Maggie and Rose.

The weight of what lay before him was nearly stifling. It was not as if he had never managed an estate. He had spent the past five years helping his friend do just that. It was just that he had never expected to not only manage his family's estate but also to take on the care of two youngsters. Why had his brother not chosen someone else to see to his daughters' care? Why must it be him?

Stuart swung down from his horse in front of a fine-looking home. It had four chimneys and two rows of windows. The entry was covered by a portico, and the shrubbery that bordered the walkway was well-tended. Aaron had most certainly done very well for himself.

The door before him was flung open before Stuart had even walked half the distance between his horse and the house.

"Stuart!" Aaron shouted as he sprinted from the house.

The sight brought a smile to Stuart's lips. It was just like his younger brother to be less than sedate. Stuart could not remember a time when Aaron had moved at anything less than a trot.

"I did not expect you for another hour!"

"And yet, you knew I was here almost before I did," Stuart teased.

Aaron laughed. "I set myself up near the window to read today so I would not miss your arrival. It seemed quite out of place for you to be greeted by a servant and not your brother."

"Especially now that you are my only brother," Stuart said.

Aaron threw his arms around Stuart and pulled him into a firm embrace. "I think I have been your only brother for several years now." His voice, unlike his actions, was soft, bordering on tender.

"I suppose you have been. I have not written much more to Broderick than was required." After what Broderick had done, one would think it would be an easy task not to write to him, but one would be wrong. There had been many times Stuart had wanted to engage in the intimacy he had shared with his brother before Sarah, but trust had been broken in a most irreparable way.

"I know. I heard."

"Broderick spoke about me?" That was surprising. Broderick had not been the sort of gentleman to confide in anyone about anything. He had been much more prone to keeping his own counsel.

"I was his parson, not just his little brother. He has repented many times for his treatment of you." Aaron held Stuart by the shoulders as if he were not yet ready to let go of him.

"Never to me," Stuart whispered. "Not one word of regret or apology ever passed between him and me."

"I know that, too." Finally, Aaron released his hold on Stuart and motioned toward the door.

Stuart held his place, not daring to move forward. "Are they here?"

Aaron nodded. "In the nursery." He smiled. "Did you know I have a nursery? It is just recently created. Now, I have only to find a wife to help me fill it."

"You could keep Rose and Maggie."

"No, I could not. They are yours. They belong at Wellworth Abbey with you, for it is their home. They have lost enough. I would not dream of taking them from their home for any longer than was necessary for you to arrive." He once again motioned toward the house. "Come. You must meet them."

"Now?" Panic surged through Stuart. He was not ready for this.

"No, but soon. They should be resting for another half hour."

Slowly, on leaden feet, Stuart made his way into the house. He was just divesting himself of his hat and running a hand through his hair when he noticed a pair of eyes watching him.

His eyes held the curious child's brown ones. He imagined that he looked just as interesting and unusual to her as she did to him. "Good afternoon, Miss Alford."

The young girl crept out of her hiding place behind the newel post halfway up the stairs where they turned to the left, and Stuart's breath left him in a mighty rush. Aaron had said the girls resembled their mother, but Stuart had not expected to be faced with a perfect miniature of Sarah.

"Are you my uncle?" the child asked.

"He is, indeed," Aaron answered. "Stuart, this is Maggie, who should be in the nursery, but I suppose her excitement was too great?"

Maggie nodded her reply though her eyes never left Stuart and his eyes never left her. Her lips tipped up into a shaky smile. "You look like Papa."

"We were twins," Stuart answered.

"I know. Papa told me." She came down one step closer to him.

"Did he?"

She nodded and wound one strand of her wavy brown locks around her finger. "He said I would like you."

"Did he?" Stuart asked for a second time. This young girl was not shy and retiring. That was a relief. He had feared meeting inquisitive children who would hate him for taking their father's place and, therefore, would not say a word.

"Why did he think you would like Uncle Stuart?" Aaron asked when Maggie only nodded in reply to Stuart's question.

"Because," she began, looking away from Stuart and toward Aaron, "because he liked him, and I always like what Papa likes." She sank down on the step she was on. "I hope I like you." Her slender shoulders drooped as if they could no longer stay upright. The sight tugged at Stuart's heart.

"I hope you do, too," he agreed.

Aaron nudged him forward, and he approached the steps. "I think Uncle Aaron was going to make me a cup of tea. Do you think you would like to join us?"

"May I?" she asked Aaron eagerly.

Stuart would have to remember that this child enjoyed teatime.

"I believe I can allow that," Aaron said.

"Can Rose come, too?"

"Is she sleeping?"

Maggie's face scrunched. "Maybe."

"Then, I think it is best if just you joined us. Besides, it might be easier for Uncle Stuart to meet just one of you at a time. You and Rose only have one new relation to meet, and Uncle Stuart has two."

Maggie cut a sidelong glance at Stuart. "We are not scary," she whispered to Aaron.

Stuart pressed his lips together to keep from chuckling. Little did this youngster know that she and her yet unseen sister were absolutely terrifying to a gentleman who had only ever had to tend to his own needs.

"No, you are not, but you are new. And would it not be fun to be able to tell Rose about Uncle Stuart before she meets him? You know how timid she can be."

An eyebrow arched and Maggie's little lips pursed to the side. The corridor stood silent for a moment before she rose from the stairs, squared her shoulders, and, with lifted chin, said, "I believe you are correct. Rose always likes it when I can tell her how someone is before she meets them."

Stuart stepped backward to allow Maggie to pass by him, but instead, she stopped in front of him.

"May I show you to the parlour?" She held out a hand that only trembled slightly.

"I would like that very much." Stuart took her hand. How small it felt in his! "May I tell you a secret?" he asked as they walked the short distance to the sitting room.

Maggie glanced at him with curious eyes and nodded.

"I am nervous," he whispered. If she was going to be brave and offer her hand to a stranger on her sister's behalf, how could he not also be courageous enough to admit that she and her sister were not the only ones who were anxious?

She blinked and her eyes grew wide. "Why?"

"The sofa," Aaron whispered behind him.

"Because I have never taken care of children before." He led Maggie to the sofa as his brother had suggested. "I have cared for estates and friends... and brothers." He darted a look at Aaron. "However, I have never cared for young ladies such as yourself and your sister."

She climbed onto the sofa and arranged herself in the middle. Her legs poked out over the edge, for she was not able to both place her back against the back of the piece of furniture and bend her knees over the edge. Again, Stuart was struck by how small this person, who had been left to his care, was.

"It is not hard," she assured him when he sat down. "We have Miss Leslie – she is our governess. Father always said she knew what to do, and she does."

There was so much trust that was given willingly by this young child. It seemed that she believed everything her father had told her and was willingly compliant with everything her governess told her to do.

"Surely, there must be something I must do?" he questioned.

She shook her head. "I do not know. Papa just

did things." Her shoulders lifted and lowered in a shrug.

He looked at Aaron who only smiled. Very well, if the fellow was not going to be a help here, Stuart would approach Maggie as he would anyone with whom he needed to form a long-lasting working relationship. "I know. How about if you tell me one thing I must do for you and one I must do for Rose that will make our lives together enjoyable. I will promise to attempt to do that thing, and when I feel ready for another, I will ask. Do you think that might work?"

She studied him for a moment before nodding while wearing a puzzled expression.

"You do not need to tell me right now. Just when you think of it," Stuart assured her.

"How was your trip?" Aaron inserted.

"It was good." Stuart's brow furrowed as he looked at his brother. It seemed a rather abrupt change of topics.

"The weather was good?"

"It was."

"Did you ride the whole way or did you spend some time in your carriage?" Aaron's lips turned up as if he already knew the answer to that question.

"I rode. I planned to enter the carriage if it rained, but we were fortunate and, though there was a grey day or two, it did not rain while we were travelling."

"Maggie likes to ride."

"Do you?" Stuart asked.

Maggie's head bobbed up and down. "Rose does not. She is afraid of the horse."

"Broderick purchased a gentle mare for the girls about a year ago. He was just helping Maggie learn to ride before his accident. Rose had not yet allowed him to do more than ride in front of him."

"I can ride by myself," Maggie inserted.

"All by yourself?"

"With her father walking alongside," Aaron added.

"I am sure I could do it by myself." Maggie folded her arms.

Stuart would have to remember that Miss Maggie Alford had a streak of independence running through her. He could understand that. He had always been so himself. How many times had he gotten into an argument with Broderick about not needing his brother's help? More times than he cared to attempt to count.

Broderick had taken his position of eldest to heart and had decided that a few minutes of life outside of a womb longer than Stuart gave him the right to tell Stuart what to do and how to do it. And yet, Stuart had loved him. Looking up at the ceiling, he drew and released a breath. He had thought the feeling was mutual until his brother had stolen Sarah from him.

"Did you ride past Pemberley?" Aaron asked. He was watching Stuart carefully.

"I did. It looked as if Darcy is home for the summer."

"He and his wife are in residence."

"Yes, you mentioned he had married."

"He has one of his wife's sisters with him for the summer."

"I like Miss Bennet," Maggie said.

"Have you met her?" Stuart's gaze shifted from his brother to Maggie.

"Yes," she said with a laugh as if his question was the silliest one she had ever heard, and he supposed it might be. How would she know if Miss Bennet was nice if she had not met her?

"Miss Bennet likes to sketch."

Stuart looked at his brother again. How was that information supposed to be helpful?

Maggie pulled her feet under her and turned toward Stuart. "She draws houses," she said as if it was the most exciting thing in the world.

"Just houses?"

Maggie shrugged. "I think so. She does not like drawing people or horses."

"Does she draw flowers?"

Maggie's head tipped. "I did not ask."

"Maybe you can ask her tomorrow before you go home," Aaron said.

A small frown settled on Maggie's expression. "But she is not done with her picture."

"I am certain Uncle Stuart would allow Miss Bennet to call on you to show you her picture."

Maggie's shoulders sagged. "But I cannot watch her if I am not here."

"The time has come for you to go home."

Maggie sighed and nodded.

"Do you think," Stuart asked, "that Miss Bennet is the sort of lady who would like to draw a picture of Wellworth Abbey?"

Trepidation filled Aaron's eyes. Was Miss Bennet not so nice as Maggie thought? Why would the mention of asking her to draw Wellworth Abbey make his brother looks so worried?

"I suppose we can ask her," he answered cautiously.

"Oh, can we?" Maggie bounced lightly where she sat.

"She may not be able to, even if she wants to," Aaron warned.

Ah! Aaron was afraid to disappoint Maggie. Stuart would need to remember to think about things like that now. There was so much he did not know about children. If he had come home once or twice over the past two years since Sarah died, perhaps he would know more about his nieces than he did. Aaron truly would have been the better brother to take the place of Maggie and Rose's father.

"But," Aaron continued, "when Uncle Stuart comes to collect you tomorrow, he can ask her."

"Will you?" Maggie was all eagerness again.

"Miss Bennet will be here?"

Maggie nodded. "She only did not come today because you were coming."

"Otherwise, she would have been sitting on the

knoll drawing," Aaron added. "Miss Leslie takes Maggie and Rose out to visit her."

"And then she and Miss Darcy come home with us and have tea."

"How is Miss Darcy?" Stuart asked Aaron.

"Will you ask Miss Bennet? Please?" Apparently, Maggie was not about to allow him to change the subject.

"If she is here, I will ask."

Maggie's face lit with pleasure. "Thank you, Uncle Stuart. Papa was right. I like you." She folded her hands in her lap, looking quite content. "Miss Darcy is pretty."

"I have not seen her in years so I would not know," Stuart replied.

"Uncle Aaron thinks she is pretty."

That, Stuart knew. "Does he?"

Aaron shook his head while Maggie nodded emphatically.

"He told me so."

"What else did he tell you about Miss Darcy?"

"He thinks she is very proper and..." She tapped her lower lip with a finger. It was so reminiscent of the expression her mother had often used when pretending she did not know something. He closed his eyes.

"She has a very nice horse."

Stuart chuckled. Horses were, it seemed, of great importance to Maggie.

"Her dresses are pretty, too, and her hats," Maggie continued.

"Uncle Aaron thinks all those things about Miss Darcy?"

Maggie's brow furrowed. "I have not asked."

Stuart turned to Aaron. "Do you agree with Maggie?"

"I would be a fool not to," he said pointedly before rising to pour the tea. "Maggie, will you see if Rose would like some tea?"

The child agreed and scooted out of the room.

"Broderick was no fool in choosing you," Aaron said once she was gone from the room. "Maggie needs you. Rose does, too, but Maggie?" He shook his head. "She is so much like you. Broderick always said so. You will do well."

"I hope you are right," Stuart muttered. He still did not feel equal to the challenge of guiding two young girls, but he was at least feeling more comfortable than he had been before.

Chapter 2

Mary Bennet gathered her drawing supplies into her arms and prepared to exit Mr. Darcy's carriage. The sky was a vibrant blue today with just a few traces of pure white fluffy clouds. It was just the sort of day she liked best – one filled with sun and drawing and free from younger sisters.

The absence of those younger sisters was perhaps the absolute best part of her trip to Derbyshire with her aunt and uncle – not that the trip lacked in reasons to enjoy it. It was just that enjoying all the wonderful bits of the trip would be harder if she had a younger sister or two with her.

Kitty would not have been a poor travelling companion, Mary thought as she handed her things to Mrs. Annesley, who had already exited the carriage, but Lydia would have been unbearable. While Kitty could have been coaxed into spending time writing stories while Mary sketched all the lovely buildings she saw, Lydia would have only been content and reasonably quiet if she were dancing or shopping. How a lady floated through life with so few serious thoughts in her head was beyond Mary's capabilities to understand. Yet, somehow, Lydia managed to do it!

Having alighted onto the ground, Mary straightened her clothing before retrieving her things from Mrs. Annesley.

Another wonderful thing about not having younger sisters with her on this trip was that she was the only Miss Bennet and there were no others besides her married sister Elizabeth with whom to compare her. She was not so overly plain when stood next to Elizabeth, but, when placed next to her eldest sister Jane or either of her two youngest sisters, she was downright forgettable.

While she did not entirely mind being forgotten on occasions – such as when her mother was pushing one of her sisters toward some unmarried gentleman with a reasonable fortune – now was not one of those times. Both of her elder sisters had married well, and her next youngest sister would be just as well-married before harvest began. That left just her and Lydia as unwed Bennets.

At nineteen and a half years old, Mary felt it was time for her to seriously contemplate marriage. There were no gentlemen who interested her in such a fashion near her home of Longbourn, and she had lost her chance to visit town during the season due to a trifling illness. There would not be another season for months, and knowing her mother, it would be Lydia who would be put forward as the best choice to visit Aunt and Uncle Gardiner in town. Mary would be placed on the shelf and consigned to the position of companion to the mistress of Longbourn, and there she would remain until some dour-looking gentleman came along. Only then, would she be presented as a possible wife because Mama had often said that Mary was destined to live a dull but serious life – likely as a parson's wife, and once Mama thought something to be true, there was little hope of shaking that fact from her mind.

Mary smiled as she turned from the carriage to look at the parsonage she was about to draw. She would not mind marrying a parson if he were as handsome and affable as Mr. Aaron Alford.

"Do not forget the blankets, John," Mrs. Anneseley instructed the footman who had been assigned as their escort. "And the picnic basket. I dare say a treat will be welcome soon." She smiled. "I have packed enough for our young visitors and you as well, John."

Mrs. Annesley was the sweetest lady Mary had ever met, for she was always watching for ways to make those around her feel at ease and welcome. Sometimes, she did her calming and cheering work through the faintest of smiles shared with a maid, and other times, her method included a picnic basket, filled with tantalizing morsels of food, to share with one and all – regardless of station.

"I wonder if the young Miss Alfords like their uncle," Georgiana Darcy said.

Mary had found Miss Darcy – or Georgiana, as she insisted upon being called – to be what the perfect younger sister should be. Interesting but quiet. Happy but not boisterous. Eager to be part of a party but without the compulsion to be the center of attention.

"I hope they do, for if they do not, it will make for a trying transition," Mrs. Annesley replied. "It will be challenging enough as it is."

Georgiana did not reply other than to sigh as if she completely understood, which, Mary knew, she did, for Georgiana had lost both of her parents just as the Alford children had. However, Georgiana had been left to the care of her brother and a cousin, both of whom she had known all her life. To Mary, it seemed that young Maggie and Rose faced a greater challenge since neither of them had ever met the uncle who was now their guardian.

"Why has Mr. Alford never come home to visit?" she asked. "Was it his occupation that kept him away?"

Mrs. Annesley shook her head. "That is not what I heard it was, but I am not given to gossip."

Mary opened her mouth to ask a further question but closed it straight away as an image of her mother and Lady Lucas whispering and clucking over some delicious tale flitted across her mind. She would rather die from curiosity than become part of that picture.

"It was a broken heart," Georgiana whispered. "But I cannot say more. It would not be right."

"Oh! How sad," Mary muttered. That little bit of information had only helped to fan the flames of her curiosity rather than douse them. Why must doing the right thing be so hard? "I do hope that Mr. Alford's heartbreak will not make his coming home now to take care of his nieces harder than it already will be."

"He will love them," Mrs. Annesley assured her. "I dare say that I would be hard-pressed to name two more charming children."

Mary could not agree with that more. Maggie and Rose Alford had been all that was polite, even if they were inquisitive. She found she quite liked them and looked forward to seeing them each time she came to work on her drawing of the parsonage and its garden. In fact, it was because of them that she had been in no rush to complete her sketch. She would miss them tomorrow.

"Loving a child can do a lot to heal a broken heart," Mrs. Annesley added. "I should know. Though I had no children of my own when Mr. Annesley passed, I was fortunate enough to find a place caring for one of the best children in the world."

"I am not a child," Georgiana said with a laugh.

"No, you are not, but you are amongst the best young ladies I have met."

"I have not always been so," Georgiana said.

"Indeed, I was quite a trial for my father and brother at times."

"You were?" Mary could not imagine Georgiana being anything other than obliging and proper.

"I like to have my way now and again." She wound her arm around Mary's. They had formed a burgeoning friendship over the past two weeks since Mary had arrived at Pemberley. "However, I have learned that my way is not always the best way."

"Could you teach that to my youngest sister?" Mary asked dryly, causing Georgiana to laugh.

"I am certain she will come to know it as she grows older."

"You say that as if you are older than she is," Mary said.

"I am," Georgiana retorted.

"By three months! That is not much."

"It is enough. It truly does not take a terribly long period of time to learn something like that. It just takes experience. I just hope your sister learns it in a less tragic fashion than I did." She added the last part in a whisper.

"How – no, I will not ask," Mary said. That image

of her mother and Lady Lucas was too fresh in her mind.

"You may at some point, if you wish," Georgiana let go of Mary's arm and claimed a spot on the blanket John had spread on the ground.

Mary sat down next to her, arranged herself carefully so that she could prop her notebook on her knees, and unrolled her packet of pencils and other drawing supplies next to her. Then, though she dearly wished to ask Georgiana about her secret, she pushed the thought out of her mind to concentrate on her page and the house in front of her while Georgiana and Mrs. Annesley read books and John leaned against a nearby tree. She would ask Georgiana about her painful lesson in a more private location – one which was away from footmen and possible little girl visits.

Some minutes later, she was just looking up to study a chimney top when she saw two Mr. Alfords approaching. The one she knew, Mr. Aaron Alford, waved a greeting. She lifted her hand in response and then put her pencil in her case.

"Do not get up," the younger Mr. Alford called as he trotted up the knoll on which she sat. "Stuart and I can join you on the ground."

Stuart, who must be the elder of the two Mr. Alfords, had not changed his pace and seemed content to allow his younger brother to arrive ahead of him. Mary wondered if it had always been so. She knew that, in her family, Lydia was always the first to gallop off to do something, and rarely, if ever, did any of her sisters run along with her. Even Kitty would follow in a more ladylike fashion. It was just how Lydia was. Exuberance poured from her in streams or, more precisely, like loud, babbling brooks that hopped here and there. While Mary did not enjoy such energy in the form of her youngest sister, she had to admit that it was not so off-putting in a handsome gentleman like Mr. Aaron Alford. Her eyes flitted back to the younger Mr. Alford who was planting himself near Mrs. Annesley.

Oh, she knew he was not for her. He was far too handsome to wish to court a plain lady like herself and, added to that, he paid much closer attention to Georgiana than he did her. However, it was fun to pretend.

"Miss Darcy, Miss Bennet, Mrs. Annesley," Mr. Aaron Alford said, "I would like you to meet my older brother, Stuart."

"It is a pleasure." Mr. Alford bowed his greeting and then sat down but just on the edge of the blanket as if he were imposing on a private gathering. "I would not have recognized you if I had passed you in a crowd, Miss Darcy. You have changed a great deal in five years."

"I was only a child the last time I saw you. I would be extraordinarily surprised if you said I looked the same as I did when I was twelve," she replied. "You, however, look very much as I remember you."

"I suppose seeing Broderick made it difficult to forget how I looked."

Georgiana laughed lightly. "Indeed," she replied before sobering and adding, "I am deeply sorry for your loss."

Mr. Alford nodded his acceptance of her words but said nothing.

"Broderick and Stuart were twins," Mr. Aaron Alford explained to Mary.

"Forgive me," Mr. Alford said. "I should have explained that." He had removed his hat and was running the rim of it between his fingers. He was most certainly not as at ease as his brother. However, he was just as handsome, if not more so.

"I am sorry for your loss as well," Mary said. "I know I did not know your brother, but I cannot imagine the sorrow of losing one of my sisters."

"I pray you do not have to discover it for years," he replied.

"And I hope your prayer is granted," Mary returned.

He ran a hand through his hair again. "Is it lying flat now?" he asked her in a whisper.

She blinked. "Is what lying flat?"

"My hair. You have been staring at it since I sat down."

Mortification coursed through Mary. She had never been caught staring at a handsome face by the owner of said handsome face before. It was not that she had not stared. It was just that she had never been noticed.

"Have I?" she managed to say. "I did not mean to be."

"Miss Bennet has an artist's eye," Mr. Aaron Alford said.

"I would not say that," Mary replied, pulling her eyes away from the elder brother to look at the younger one.

"I have seen the sketches in your book and heard

your praise from my nieces. Therefore, I am afraid, Miss Bennet, that you are going to have to accept it as true."

She shook her head. "While it is true that I can sketch a house reasonably well, the ability to draw straight lines, make a few smudges for shadows, and swirl the occasional twisting branch of a tree on paper neither equates to me having an artistic eye nor to my being an artist. I am simply a lady who likes to sketch."

"Then, you do not see beauty in the world around you?" Mr. Aaron Alford pressed.

"Does not everyone?"

He chuckled. "You seem set on not admitting to being an accomplished artist."

"I am until such time as it is true. I try diligently not to prevaricate."

"Then," said the other Mr. Alford, "if you were not taking note of hair that was out of place and you were also not looking at me with the idea of capturing my likeness, why were you staring at me?"

Mary swallowed. How did she answer that honestly without saying she was admiring his features? "I have never seen you before." That was true.

"Am I to assume that you stare at every stranger you meet?" His lips were curled up the tiniest bit. Clearly, he was beginning to feel at ease enough to tease and torment.

"Yes, that is precisely what you are to assume for it is the truth. I do tend to observe new acquaintances closely upon meeting. It helps me remember them." She picked up her pencil.

"That must make meeting people a trifle awkward."

"Only if they notice," she replied with a smile before turning her attention back to her drawing as if she were actually going to be able to do much more than pretend to draw. She replaced her pencil in the case. Pretending to draw would be a lot like prevaricating, would it not be?

"Well, now, that my brother has made this first meeting somewhat uncomfortable, we had a purpose in coming to see you that must be dealt with directly." He tilted his head toward the side garden of the parsonage. "Maggie and Rose will soon join us." He gave his elder brother a severe glare that made Mary wonder what the elder Mr. Alford had done.

"Maggie is reluctant to return home before your

drawing of the parsonage is complete, Miss Bennet," Mr. Alford said. "I wanted to ask you before she was with you if you would be so kind as to call at Wellworth Abbey to show her the completed drawing and to create a sketch of Wellworth."

"You wish for Mary to draw your home?" Georgiana said in surprise. "It is a rather large building. It would take some time."

"I know." He ran the edge of his hat through his fingers again. "I may have suggested the idea yesterday when Maggie was upset about having to leave here. I did not think about how such a suggestion might cause her further disappointment." He looked at Mary. "I do understand if you will not be able to grant my whole request."

"It would take several days," Mrs. Annesley cautioned.

Several days spent at a handsome gentleman's home did not seem utterly horrid to Mary, not even if that gentleman had been rather pointed in his questioning of her moments ago.

"I cannot promise," she replied after a moment of pondering the opportunity of being able to see another handsome Alford gentleman each day. "I will have to ask Mr. Darcy if he will allow it. I cannot expect Miss Darcy and Mrs. Annesley to spend all their time escorting me to various places, so I might require a maid to be at my disposal. Nor can I expect my relations to give me up completely to my own pursuits instead of spending time with them."

He nodded and grimaced. "I did not think of those things either. This is all so new."

His words tugged at her heart. She knew very well how it was to feel out of place. She had spent a good portion of her life feeling just so. "I am certain something can be arranged. If I cannot commit to drawing your home, then, perhaps there is a special toy or object that Maggie treasures that I could sketch?"

His broad shoulders sagged in what Mary hoped was relief. "I would be grateful to you for any assistance you can give me in making Maggie's new life more enjoyable."

And just like that, with the novel idea that she – Mary Bennet – and not one of her sisters, could help those who were floundering in unfamiliar waters, the need to secure a way to visit Wellworth Abbey lodged itself firmly in Mary's heart.

Chapter 3

The sun was well over the horizon before Stuart woke the next day. He could not remember a time in his life – other than five years ago – when he felt so lost and weary in his soul. But then, five years ago was the last time his world had been set on end, leaving him headed in a direction that was neither welcome nor comfortable.

Tossing his feet over the edge of the bed, Stuart sat up and looked around his room. It felt wrong to be here. This room was his father's, and then, it had also been his brother's. He would not have chosen to sleep in here last night. He would much rather have been put in his old bedchamber instead of here. At least in there, a few of the ghosts of the past would have remained outside the door. Sarah had never been in that bed.

However, this was the room to which his things

had been brought and set out, and he was the master of his family's estate. It mattered not whether he wished for such a title or not. It was his. Yet, this room, and that bed. He rubbed the back of his neck. Surely there must be a reasonable compromise that could be made. If he could just be rid of this confounded piece of furniture. His left brow arched at the thought. That just might be it.

"Do you think it would be too much bother to have my bed brought in here to replace this one?" He rose from the edge of the bed to greet Duncan, who had brought in a cup of tea.

"It is your home, sir."

Stuart nodded as he swallowed a sip of the warm beverage that, no matter where he was, was his way of greeting to the morning. "But do you think it could be done today?"

"If you say it must be, sir, then, I am certain it can be."

"And will everyone below stairs hate me if I say it must be?" He had no desire to be thought of as a demanding and grumbling sort of gentleman. But he truly could not sleep in his brother's bed for one more night.

In the reflection from the looking glass, he saw

his new valet's lips curl up in a slight smile. "I am certain, sir, from what I have heard, that you are not the sort of employer whom anyone could ever hate."

The comment made Stuart curious as to what the man could have heard about him and from whom. Most likely it was from Broderick, as that was whom this fellow had served until recently.

"I do not wish to make a poor first impression," Stuart explained.

"Changes are to be expected, sir. You must make this house your home."

That was true, and it did ease Stuart's mind somewhat.

A jug of water was tested for warmth, and then, the necessary tools for grooming were laid out on the washstand.

"I will notify the housekeeper of your desires in the least demanding way I know how, sir. Will that do?"

"That would be greatly appreciated." He answered and continued to enjoy his tea while his man made certain all was ready for Stuart to wash and dress. Stuart had requested that he be allowed to see to his own ablutions. He had not relied on a man to help him dress in years, and he was a trifle reluctant to give up such freedom.

"I will return in twenty minutes to help with anything that is needed," Duncan said before ducking out of the room.

And with that, Stuart was once again left to his own thoughts. Today, he would poke around his new study to see what sorts of books and methods of recording Broderick had used. Tomorrow, he would meet with Mr. Lidstone to hear the details of the workings of the estate. He had no doubt he would settle into the running of the estate quite well. Livestock, crops, and the like were livestock, crops, and the like – no matter whose they had been or now were. Commodities. That is what they were. Things which provided for the life of those associated with them – this life. He looked around his bedchamber. This new and unwelcomed life. That was the part which would take more work to settle into.

Stuart placed his empty cup on the table next to his chair, and rising, went to the window to survey his land. *His land.* He shook his head. This had always been his father's land to him – even when Broderick had come into his inheritance, this land had still belonged to their father in Stuart's mind. Perhaps if he had visited even once since the period of mourning for their father was over, this land upon which he now looked would feel less like his father's and more like a possession to be passed from one keeper of the estate to the next.

The view from the window was spectacular. The reminder that this was all now his was less dazzling. On the one hand, he looked forward to being his own man and making decisions as he saw fit without having to bow to the wishes of another. On the other hand, the reason for why he was now responsible for all he saw was not far from him.

"I will see it secured for the future," he promised to the memory of his father, "for Rose and Maggie," he added to the memory of his brother as he crossed to the washstand behind the screen in the corner and began to prepare for the day that lay before him.

~*~*~

"Why can I not go for a ride?" Maggie asked for the fifth time since entering the breakfast room with Rose.

Stuart had been told that the children had often broken their fast with their father, and so, in an attempt to keep things as they had been as much as possible for his young charges, he had agreed to the practice. At present, he was regretting that decision.

"I must settle into my study," he said once again. "Work before pleasure."

"But Papa rode before eating."

Maggie was exceptionally good at pouting, and Stuart had to avert his eyes to not fall prey to such a stricken expression.

"I apologize, Maggie, but today is not the day to take a morning ride. Did your Papa take you with him when he went riding?"

"No," Rose said softly with a shake of her head.

"They never went to the stables before eating, sir," Miss Leslie added with a pointed look for Maggie.

He could see why Broderick had relied on the lady so much. Miss Leslie was, he would guess, about forty years old if not a half year older. While her countenance was friendly and held the hints of being quite pretty when she was younger, her disposition was firm – kind, but firm. Maggie seemed to need just such a lady to keep her pointed in the right direction, and Rose, he could imagine, found it comforting to have such a stalwart guide.

"When did they go to the stables?"

"Just before their rest period, unless, of course, we were expecting callers."

Callers? He had not thought that Broderick would have many callers. "Did you have guests often?"

Miss Leslie smiled. "Your brother was a widower with a handsome face and estate."

Ah, yes. A single man with a fortune must be in want of a wife, must he not be? Such foolishness!

"I would expect a neighbour or two to visit you as well, sir, once the appropriate amount of time has passed," Miss Leslie answered.

Maggie's brow was furrowed as she looked between Miss Leslie and Stuart. "But those ladies do not know my uncle," she said.

"They will wish to meet him."

"Why?" Rose asked.

"Because he is their new neighbor," Miss Leslie replied.

"And because I am not married," he muttered with a shake of his head.

"There is that, too," Miss Leslie agreed.

"They have no hope," he assured her.

"Why?" Rose asked.

Stuart doubted that a three-year-old young lady would understand his reasons, but he had always disliked it when adults treated children as if they were unable to understand things. So, he wiped his mouth and looked directly at Rose. "Because I do not wish to marry."

"Ever?" Miss Leslie covered her mouth with her fingers and apologized while turning an amusing shade of red.

"Never," he assured her. "I once thought I wished to marry, but the lady proved untrue." While he now possessed that which had disqualified him from being accepted by Sarah, he had no desire to be accepted by a lady whose whole goal in life was to be the mistress of Wellworth Abbey.

"You may speak," he said to Miss Leslie who looked as if not speaking was somewhat painful.

"It is not my place."

"I assure you that I hold very loosely to what is and is not one's place." He smiled. "Perhaps when the position in which I find myself is not so new, I will hold to those divisions more firmly, but for now, I do not. I would like to hear your thoughts."

"You would?"

He nodded.

"Very well, then," she said. "I was just going to protest that not all ladies are untrustworthy and that to dismiss them all for the sin of one seems a trifle harsh."

"I prefer to think of it as safe, not harsh."

Her lashes fluttered. "I am sure you would not wish for Rose or Maggie to think that being untrustworthy is merely a result of their good fortune in being born female."

He squeezed his eyes shut. He had done it again. He really must begin thinking like a gentleman who needed to raise proper young ladies must think. He rubbed the spot between his eyes.

"No, no, I would not wish for them to think that." He smiled at Maggie and Rose. "They shall be the best, most trustworthy young ladies in all of Derbyshire."

"Like Miss Bennet and Miss Darcy?" Maggie asked.

He looked at Miss Leslie who nodded.

"Yes," he replied. "Like Miss Bennet and Miss Darcy."

"Miss Bennet is a fine reason for your uncle to

not take you riding today," Miss Leslie said. "You would not wish to be too tired to visit with her when she comes, now would you?"

Maggie sucked in a quick breath of air as her eyes grew wide and she shook her head.

"Then, I think, if your uncle will allow it, we should return to the nursery to make certain it is tidy and to do our reading before our guest arrives."

She was a godsend. Miss Leslie was just the blessing he had needed to find at Wellworth to make certain that his new position as guardian to his nieces did not end in disaster.

"Will we meet you before or after you give Miss Bennet a tour of the house?" Miss Leslie asked.

"A tour of the house?" Had he agreed to do such a thing? He did not remember it if he had.

"I apologize. I assumed you would give Miss Bennet a tour so she could decide what to sketch."

"I thought Maggie was deciding that." Was not Maggie supposed to choose an item that was special and present it for Miss Bennet to draw?

"If that is how you wish it to be," Miss Leslie said.

"There is some refurnishing that is going to be happening today, so it might be best."

Miss Leslie's features registered her surprise at that.

"I simply wanted my old bed to sleep in," he said as if the explanation was needed, which it was not.

"I see," the governess said. "Will there be other changes?"

"Not today."

"Very good. Then, we will meet you in the drawing room in two hours." She turned to Maggie and Rose. "Miss Alford, Miss Rose."

Both girls climbed off their chairs and came to curtsey next to Stuart before leaving. However, Maggie did not move from beside him after she had dipped her curtsey.

"Uncle," she said hopefully, "I have decided my thing."

"Your thing?" What thing was she supposed to decide? Perhaps he should begin carrying a notebook to jot notes in so he could remember what he was and was not supposed to say or do.

"The thing you said to tell you that would make our life together nice."

Oh, yes, that thing. "Have you?"

She nodded and looked a bit nervous.

"And what is it?"

"May I kiss your cheek every morning after breakfast?"

"Of course." He leaned forward to present her with his cheek.

She placed the lightest peck on his skin, but he felt it to the center of his being. This young child who had only known him for a day and a half was placing her trust in him and bestowing her care without any provocation to do so – had he not only moments ago denied her wish to ride? That was not something which would endear a child to him. Broderick may have done some things which were wrong in his life, but it seemed he had also done something incredibly good in bringing up his daughters.

"Miss Rose?" Stuart asked.

Rose shook her head emphatically.

"Rose still thinks you are scary," Maggie whispered.

"Tell her that I still find her somewhat scary as well," Stuart whispered in reply.

Maggie giggled, as he knew she would. "We are not scary."

"Maybe not to someone who knows what to do with little girls, but to me, you are."

Maggie gave his cheek another kiss. "For Rose," she said and then scurried away to the door to follow Miss Leslie out of the breakfast room.

Chapter 4

Mary followed Mr. Darcy and Elizabeth as Mr. Branston, Wellworth Abbey's butler, led them to the drawing room. Georgiana was at her side, and her aunt and uncle Gardiner were behind them. She saw no need for a complete invasion of Wellworth Abbey by her relations. However, Mr. Darcy and Uncle Gardiner had not agreed, and no amount of protesting that she would not cause a scandal if she was allowed to visit Maggie and Rose with just Georgiana and Mrs. Annesley to accompany her was going to sway them.

Once again, a little sister – Kitty in this case – was interfering with what Mary wished to do. Of course, it was not actually Kitty's fault that she had found herself embroiled in scandal in the spring while in town. The scandal had been created by her betrothed, Mr. Linton. However, to a lady with younger sisters who have spent their whole lives interfering, the facts mattered little, and the blame, however unjustly it was distributed, fell on Kitty in Mary's mind.

The fact that Elizabeth had insisted she must meet her new neighbours had done little to brighten Mary's mood. It had been an argument used to help Mary see that Uncle Gardiner and Mr. Darcy were not being unreasonable. But again, the logic of it all did not matter. What mattered was that not only was a younger sister interfering with Mary's plans and desires but so was an elder sister. Could Mary not have something – anything – that was hers and hers alone? Something that would belong to neither an elder sister before her nor be passed on to a younger sister after her?

"My brother only wishes to see that you are well," Georgiana whispered. She had said that very same thing to Mary several times today.

"I know," Mary replied, just as she had every other time. And in her heart, she knew that Mr. Darcy was not attempting to destroy her life. She truly did. Be that as it may, at present, it felt somewhat as if he was. This was supposed to be her moment to shine. Now, it would not be. Elizabeth would shine. She always did. Unlike her sisters, Mary possessed no glittery bits.

"Miss Bennet!" Maggie waved from where she stood between her uncle and sister as introductions were being made.

Rose, seeing her sister was waving, followed suit.

"It seems you are very well-liked, Mary," Aunt Gardiner said with a laugh.

It did appear that way, and those two little waves began melting away the cloud of gloom that had surrounded Mary since yesterday when she had been told that the whole party from Pemberley was going to accompany her to Wellworth Abbey.

"Miss Bennet has been eagerly awaited," Mr. Alford said. "Maggie hopes to show her the nursery if she is willing. There is a chair in there that might be the best item to sketch."

"Is that so?" Mrs. Gardiner asked Maggie, who had just climbed onto the couch near her uncle and was straightening her skirt. "What makes the chair special?"

"It is the story chair."

"Stories are wonderful, are they not?" Aunt Gardiner asked.

Maggie nodded. "Papa used to read them to us sometimes. Now, Miss Leslie does."

"I would have to agree that such a chair is very special," Aunt Gardiner said.

Mary looked from Maggie to her uncle to gauge his feelings on the matter of stories and his deceased brother. He was not fully unaffected; there was a touch of sadness in his expression. She had thought yesterday that he seemed the sort to be a very doting guardian for the girls, though he had also appeared terrified of the prospect. Today, he looked a touch more at ease, though somewhat uncomfortable.

"I have just been introduced to the chair myself," he said. "I may get a turn to sit in it at some point."

Maggie smiled up at him and nodded her agreement.

Mary had never seen a child who was so ready to accept and love a stranger after having suffered so great a loss as Maggie had. She knew she would have struggled as a child to accept anyone in her father's place. Indeed, she likely still would – even if that person were not Mr. Collins but rather a handsome gentleman like Mr. Alford.

"I understand from your brother, Mr. Aaron

Alford, that you have been involved in some estate management in the south." Mr. Darcy said.

"I have been."

"Then, I imagine you feel equal to the task set before you at Wellworth?"

"As equal as any gentleman can feel when presented with an unexpected change in his future." Mr. Alford smiled at his eldest niece who had scooted closer to him.

"I only mention it," Mr. Darcy explained, "because I have some idea of what you might be facing, though I had expected to inherit so it was not such a shock for me as I am certain it is for you. I am happy to be of assistance in anything. Just send a message."

Guilt poked at Mary's conscience. It had been rather self-centered of her to think that Mr. Darcy's reason for joining her on her visit was merely on her account.

"I will keep that in mind. I do hope you were not too surprised by my request of your wife's sister and your niece," Mr. Alford addressed that part to Uncle Gardiner, "to draw something for Maggie."

"It was a surprise, but the explanation which

accompanied the request was understandable," Uncle Gardiner assured Mr. Alford.

There had been more than one set of raised eyebrows when Mary had returned to Pemberley yesterday and had, over dinner, expressed her desire to visit Wellworth Abbey. It had been thought very strange that a gentleman who was wholly unknown to her would ask her to sketch his home upon being introduced. That is, it was thought to be strange until Mary had explained how apologetic Mr. Alford had been and how he found his new situation as caretaker for two youngsters to be unsettling. Then, there had been nothing but understanding comments about the difficult place in which Mr. Alford had been placed, and the scheme to all visit Wellworth Abbey had been proposed – and protested.

The door to the drawing room opened, and Miss Leslie stepped just inside the door.

"If it is agreeable to all," Mr. Alford said, "I arranged for the girls' governess to escort Miss Bennet to the nursery so she can see the reading chair."

"That is an excellent idea." Aunt Gardiner

sounded excessively pleased by the plan. "Do you wish for anyone else to accompany you, my dear?"

Mary shook her head. "No, I am happy to go alone," she glanced at Georgiana, "unless Georgiana wishes to visit the nursery with Maggie and Rose. Do you?"

"I would like that, if it is agreeable to Miss Alford and Miss Rose."

"What do you think, Maggie?" Mr. Alford said. "Do you want both Miss Darcy and Miss Dennet to visit the nursery?"

"Oh, yes, please," the child replied.

"And what about you, Rose?"

"Yes, please," she answered.

"Then, it seems I will join you, Mary."

~*~*~

The nursery was a large and well-appointed room, but then, all the rooms, into which Mary had been able to peek while following Maggie and attempting to listen to everything the child had to say, had appeared to be discerningly decorated.

"This is where the children spend their day," Miss Leslie said, capturing Mary's attention and pulling it away from her perusal of the room. "Mrs.

Fenton, along with Harriet and Susan, see to much of their care unless there are lessons to be learned."

A pleasant-looking, plump woman with dark curls that poked out from under her cap stood just inside the nursery doorway. Two younger maids stood just behind her.

"It is a pleasure to meet you, Miss Bennet and Miss Darcy," Mrs. Fenton said when Miss Leslie had completed the introductions. "We are quite happy to be of assistance with anything, should you need it."

"Miss Bennet is going to draw the reading chair," Maggie said.

"Yes, miss, you told me. It is very exciting." The older woman smiled at Mary as if to say the excitement of the prospect of Mary drawing a chair had been spoken of more than once.

"The chair is not in here," Maggie said to Mary. "We must go into the night nursery."

"You do not read stories in the day nursery?" Georgiana asked.

"Not in the reading chair," Maggie replied as if she was somewhat shocked that such a question should need to be asked and answered.

"Where do you read in here?" Mary asked.

"At the table," Rose answered, pointing to a square table on the far side of the room near the window. One side of the table pressed up to the windowsill and on two sides there were benches facing each other across the table, while a single chair stood at the top.

"That is where we do lessons," Maggie explained.

"And make pictures," Rose added.

"And letters and numbers," Maggie said with no little amount of pride. This was not a child who disliked her lessons. "Rose does not do letters and numbers yet."

"But she will," Miss Leslie inserted. "When she is one year older, then she will begin writing her name. Just as you did at her age, and I do think she will be quite good at it. Do you not agree, Miss Alford?"

Maggie nodded.

"I was hired when Miss Alford was four and a half," Miss Leslie explained. "The late Mr. Alford wished to have me well-settled into the way of things and acquainted with his daughters before we began any lessons in earnest. He said his father had been a firm believer in relationships fostering respect and greater learning. I must say I was surprised by such thinking, but it has proven to work well here."

"It is a novel idea, I suppose." Truly, Mary had little idea of whether it was or was not. She had never really spent a great deal of time thinking about the education of children and the hiring of governesses and such. She supposed, since she had always longed to be a mother, she probably should have, but she had not. She only knew that she would one day make certain her children were well-taught. All of them. From the eldest to the youngest. They would know all their subjects and be proper. None of her children would be forgotten or overlooked.

"In my experience, it is an unusual way of thinking," Miss Leslie said. "My governess cared little about her relationship with me, and at the former home I was in, the children had no care to form an attachment with anyone who was not of their class." She held Mary's gaze. "I am being too forward. I know this. It has been a struggle all my life I am afraid. However, I think it is good for you to know these things, as you will be with us while you draw, and I do not wish for you to be surprised by our informality if you are accustomed to something more formal."

"I did not have a governess," Mary admitted. "We had only a nurse and my parents."

Miss Leslie's eyebrows raised. "No governess? Not at all?"

Mary shook her head.

"Did you have masters who came to your home?"

"No, not as one might expect. We did have a dance instructor visit a time or two, but he was no master. And there was a piano teacher who came a few times until my youngest sister spilled a glass of water on his music. She said it was an accident, but Lydia is Lydia and does not like lessons."

"Oh!" Miss Leslie looked completely at a loss for words.

"My father has his own unique ideas about education."

"I see." Still, Miss Leslie looked startled.

"I had a governess who was very kind," Georgiana said. "She kept her distance as she and my father thought was fitting of her station, but she was so kind. I loved her dearly, though I dared not display such sentiments. I would have much preferred a situation where I would not have had to conceal my affection for her." She smiled at Maggie and Rose. "I had no mother, so there were few to give me hugs. Mrs. Reynolds, our housekeeper, always made sure I received a hug every day, but we never told my father about it. Thankfully, my brother is not so rigid on such things as my father was, but then, again, my brother did not have a mother for much of his life either."

"No hugs? None?" Mary suspected she felt exactly as Miss Leslie had felt upon learning that Mary had not had a governess. How could a child be raised without an occasional embrace? She was neither her father's nor her mother's favourite, but she had never wanted for affection. Indeed, her father would still at times tell her to give her "old Papa" a hug.

"Not many," Georgiana replied.

"I will hug you," Maggie offered.

"I would like that," Georgiana said with a smile as she bent down to receive a hug not just from Maggie but also from Rose, who was not to be left out. Mary was not to be ignored either and was showered with affection as soon as Georgiana had received hers.

"The chair is through here." Miss Leslie led them to a bedroom that adjoined the day nursery.

There, near the hearth, was a rocker that was large enough to hold two adults, or one adult and two children, quite easily. A folded quilt hung over one arm of the chair and a cushion stood at an angle against the other. A doll propped against the pillow looking for all the world as if it were waiting for someone to come read to it.

"It is lovely," Mary said softly. She would love to have such a chair, but she could think of one sister who would adore this chair even more than she would – Kitty, the sister she had been blaming for today's disappointment. Mary's conscience pricked her, reprimanding her for her poor attitude and unjust feeling toward Kitty.

"May I draw it twice?" she asked.

"Twice?" Miss Leslie was once again looking startled.

"Perhaps three times," Mary adjusted. "One picture for Maggie. One for Rose. And one for my sister Kitty. She is getting married soon, and I know she would love a chair like this." She walked over to the piece of furniture and ran a finger along its curved back. "She likes to write stories sometimes, and I can just see her sitting in a chair like this with her children, reading them a story she has written for them."

Mary had always known Kitty liked writing stories. She had seen her scribbling things in a notebook and then hiding it away before Lydia saw her. One did not allow Lydia access to things that were special, for Lydia was well-known amongst her sisters for pinching things she wanted for herself. She was better about it now than she was when she was little, but she would still borrow things without asking, simply because she insisted that is what sisters did for one another. Inwardly, Mary groaned. She would be the only one from whom Lydia would be borrowing things now that their other sisters were married or nearly so.

"I think three pictures would be perfect," Miss Leslie said, "unless Miss Alford thinks otherwise."

Maggie's lips were pursed as if she was considering it.

Mary quite liked how the decision had been deferred to the child who found this chair so special, rather than the matter just being decided while the child's thoughts and feelings were ignored.

"I will make each drawing special for the person who will receive it," Mary said to Maggie. "For instance, if I draw this chair for my sister, I would put her blanket on the end and her pillow here, and instead of a doll, I would put a book here. Maybe open, maybe closed. I am not certain which, but it would be a book here. And for Rose, I will make sure that her favourite toy is here in place of your doll."

Maggie smiled. "You knew it was my doll?"

Mary nodded. "I did. It has a blue flower on its dress just like your dress did the first day I met you." That little bit of blue had been a tiny speck of brightness on Maggie's grey mourning clothes. The symbolism of life amid darkness had been one which captured Mary's mind and had inspired a few sketches of shadows that faded into flowers.

Maggie's smile grew wider as she nodded. "I would like you to draw it three times."

"I will not need to do all the drawing here," Mary cautioned. "I do not know how many times I will be allowed to come visit, and the first drawing can be copied with small alterations being made to personalize it for the other recipients. Do you understand?" She did not want Maggie to expect her to be at Wellworth Abbey every day.

"I do," Maggie said, though her tone did not say she was pleased with what she was being told. "Do you want to sit in it?"

The offer surprised Mary. "May I? It is incredibly special."

"You may," Maggie said proudly.

"Must I tell a story if I sit in it?" Mary asked. "I do not have one to read, but I could tell you something about myself if you want."

Maggie looked at Miss Leslie. "Can she? Please?"

"So long as it is not a long story and Miss Darcy and I can make ourselves comfortable on your bed."

"Please! Please!" Rose bounced on her toes.

Mary settled into the middle of the rocking chair while each of her two little friends climbed up next to her – one on each side. This was another reason to find a husband, for with a husband came children. Little people who would look to her for stories and comfort and anything else they needed. The desire for that feeling squeezed Mary's heart, begging for fulfillment. For so long she had just been Mary – too old for some things and too young for others, always stuck by herself in the middle and alone.

"Now, what shall I tell you? Let me think for a moment." She tapped her lip and allowed her mind to wander to her childhood. There was likely something there that could be shared. Ah! Yes. She would tell them about the time she got locked in the dairy when hiding from her little sisters. That would be a fun tale.

Chapter 5

Stuart stood behind his desk and rubbed his sore neck. The books all looked to be in order. It had only taken him a day and a half to review what needed reviewing in them. He would have no difficulties paying for any of the laborers who had been contracted to do work on the house, nor would he need to worry about the funds needed for the day-to-day and year-to-year expenses. Wellworth Abbey was in good repair both physically and financially. His father and his brother had done an exceptional job seeing to the management of the estate.

It was almost disappointing. The challenge of finding a few missing pounds or a way to retrench was far easier and more to his liking than deciding what colour to paint the small drawing room behind the library. What did it matter what colour it was or if the furniture was modern or from the last century or earlier? The room was only used by family on occasion and rarely during the day. Candlelight did little to show off the colour and shape of the furnishings in the room. At least, that was how he thought about it.

He drew a breath. It had to be decided. The workers could not move ahead without a decision. He would just have to go look at the room once again, remember his mother sitting in her favourite chair, and then pick a colour.

This house was too full of memories. Many of them were good and had always brought a smile to his face when they came to mind – until now. Now, when the weight of the walls and foundations of this grand home sat on his shoulders. Now, when the portrait of the lady he had asked to marry him and had thought was promised to him hung between his brother's portrait and one of their two daughters.

If only he could scold his current melancholy mood away. Then, things might be more bearable. He paused in front of Sarah's portrait. How had he been so deceived as to think she loved him? She had never made it a secret that she intended to marry for wealth and position, but being a love-sick swain, he had imagined her affection for him was genuine and strong enough to sway her away from a fortune that was larger than he had ever thought he had a hope of providing.

He studied Sarah's image for a few moments. He had avoided this part of the long gallery until now because he had feared what emotions it might conjure within him. However, as he looked at Sarah's likeness, it did not tug at his heart and make him long to be with her as it would have five years ago. Honestly, aside from feeling foolish and abused, he felt nothing for her. Not even anger, he realized with a start. When had that emotion slipped away? He had been certain he would carry anger for the remainder of his life because of her, and he had to say that it was a welcome relief to know that he would not.

However, as he stepped in front of his brother's portrait, he knew the bitterness he felt toward Sarah was not entirely gone. This painting was the first one that had ever been done of Broderick without Stuart at his side. This image smote Stuart's heart with great force. To his mind, it was the embodiment of loneliness – a man without his shadow, as it were. The flames of anger at Sarah flickered briefly within him. The isolation he had felt for years due to his separation from Broderick had not been a small injury to bear. He shook his head. It was not all her doing. He had chosen to cut himself off from his brother.

"Did she trick you as she tricked me?" he asked his brother's image. "Or did she truly love you?"

Stuart had spent the better portion of a year hoping that Broderick and Sarah would be miserable with one another. It had seemed a just punishment for their lack of consideration for his feelings in their twisted tale. Broderick was not unaware of the fact that Stuart was enamoured with Sarah. No one who knew anything about Stuart was unaware of his feelings regarding Miss Vernon, as she had been known then.

Perhaps Aaron would know if Broderick had been happy. Broderick's letters had always painted a happy family life, but it could have been a lie. Stuart had always made certain to make his letters to Broderick sound as if he were completely content with his life – and he was, to a point.

The sound of someone in the long gallery caught his attention.

"Miss Bennet," he called before she could scoot away.

She froze and turned toward him slowly.

"Did you need something?" he asked.

"No, I was just on my way home. To Pemberley." She motioned toward the stairs behind her. Her eyes left his and fell on the paintings that hung near her.

"Would you like a tour of the long gallery?" He was certain that was why she was here. How could he blame her? Whether she accepted the fact that she was an artist or not, he suspected she found the draw to view portraits and paintings to be a strong one.

A smile touched her features. She really was an attractive young lady when she smiled. Not that she was unattractive when she was not smiling, but her smile certainly added a compelling brightness to her eyes and features.

"You would not mind if I looked? Miss Leslie thought you would not, but..." She shrugged. "I did not wish to disturb you."

"I am just putting off what needs to be done. I would be most happy for a reason to put it off for a bit longer." He would much rather introduce a pretty young lady to his relations than pick décor.

"You do not strike me as someone who puts things off, Mr. Alford," she said as she joined him in front of Broderick's picture. "Oh, my!" She looked from the painting on the wall to Stuart and back. "This is your brother?"

Stuart nodded.

"It is as if you are standing in front of a mirror," she said as she studied Broderick with the same intensity with which she had studied Stuart upon their first meeting. She had not been prevaricating about the fact that she was a keen observer of people.

"We were identical. My mother insisted that I always wore something with yellow on it when I was an infant until she could tell Broderick and I apart. There are differences, though they are slight and not all in features."

She turned toward him again. "Did the artist straighten your brother's nose?"

He chuckled. "No, a horse un-straightened mine."

Her eyes grew wide with horror.

"It was unpleasant. I would advise you not to

stand behind a horse when it is agitated and prone to kick. Not even if your brother promises you a half-crown. It is not worth the pain and loss of blood."

Her face twisted into an expression that said she was very unwilling to hear anything further about how a horse had broken his nose. It was so far from the serious expressions he had seen her wear in their short acquaintance that he had to admit it piqued his curiosity about who Miss Bennet truly was. He had learned five years ago to never accept someone for how they appeared to be when he first met them. Indeed, he often questioned a person's true identity for a long time after the first meeting. He had Sarah to thank for that.

"Mother was not pleased, and I did not get my half-crown for the effort. Broderick was not willing to part with it after the correction he received from Father, although I dare say his backside did not cause him nearly as much discomfort as my face caused me. Thankfully, Father decided a broken nose and swollen eyes were enough punishment for my foolishness."

"Oh." She turned her eyes back to Broderick's picture. It was a moment before she spoke again.

"Did your brother often challenge you to do things?"

"We were competitive. Everything was a challenge to us. I was always trying to best him, and he was always attempting to best me. Most of it was in good fun."

"But not all of it?" Her head was tipped, and she was studying him again.

"No," he admitted. "Not all of it."

"And that is why you have not been home in years?"

She was not lacking in logic.

He nodded. "It is, but we will leave it at that."

Her eyes grew wide again. "Forgive me. I was not attempting to pry into things that are not my business." Her cheeks were rosy. "I forgot myself."

"There is nothing to forgive. We are all curious."

"No, it was wrong." Her serious look was back.

"I am not offended."

"Thank you." She turned her attention to the painting next to Broderick's. "This must be Maggie's and Rose's mother. She looks just like them."

"She does. And that is a portrait of Maggie and Rose when Rose was nearly one. It was done a year before their mother died."

She sent him a curious look.

"She and her son died in childbirth."

Miss Bennet gasped. "How dreadful! Your poor brother." Her hand lay on her heart. "And Maggie and Rose." She shook her head sadly. "To lose both their mother and father at such a young age."

"Broderick was killed in an accident. He was helping to repair a roof and slipped on the tiles."

"Oh," she sighed as if in agony. "I have no words to describe the sorrow I feel for you, your other brother, and your nieces."

He withdrew his handkerchief from his pocket and handed it to her. She may not have had the words, but she most certainly had the tears to express herself.

She dabbed at the tears in her eyes. "I would ask you about your parents, but I fear I will become a watering pot if I do. I do not deal well with death," she added softly as if it was some dreadful weakness.

"I am not convinced that anyone with a heart does," he assured her. "My parents are here." He motioned to their right. "Illness of different sorts took them from us. I was sixteen when our mother died of cancer, and father's heart took him from us when I was twenty-three."

"So much loss," she murmured as she studied his parents' portrait. "And this is you and your brothers?"

"Yes."

"Was it horribly trying to sit for the painting?"

"Excessively. Have you never sat for a portrait?"

"I did once. My mother insisted that there be a painting somewhere at Longbourn that marked her daughters' existence for posterity's sake." She handed him his handkerchief. A hint of amusement shone in her still misty eyes. "It was dreadful and had to be done in stages. There were five of us to position just so. I and my two eldest sisters were capable of being bored for extended periods of time. My two youngest sisters were not. In fact, I dare say my youngest sister is still incapable of the feat."

"Four sisters? No brothers?"

Miss Bennet shook her head. "Much to my mother's disappointment and continued fear, no." She looked back at the portrait of Stuart, Broderick, and Aaron. "I hope for the sake of Maggie and Rose that the estate is not entailed."

Ah! Her home must be entailed.

"Although, I suppose if it is, there is still hope." She turned to him brightly. "You could marry and have a son," she said and then her face seemed to catch fire as it turned a brilliant shade of red. "I am not... I did not mean..." she stammered. "Forgive me."

"You are not putting your name forward for the role of Mrs. Alford?" he teased before he could think better of it.

"No. No. I am not," she said quickly and then added, "Not that it would be a horrible thing –" her lips clamped shut and she covered her face with her hands.

She was easily flustered and apparently as concerned with propriety as she had appeared to be when he first met her. He was quite certain he had never met another young lady quite like her.

"I am jesting. I did not think you were putting yourself forward."

Her face remained hidden by her hands as she shook her head.

"You were attempting to help me see that not all was lost."

Her hands moved slowly away from her face, and he handed her his handkerchief again.

"Can you forgive me for teasing you?"

She nodded as she dried her eyes.

"Since I have, through my thoughtless words, caused you embarrassment, would you like to know what horrendous task I am avoiding?"

Her brow furrowed. "Perhaps?" There was a wariness in her reply.

That was a first. He had never met anyone who had looked at him in such an uncertain fashion. He must be making quite the impression.

"I have to tell the painters what colour to paint a room. Broderick has two colours listed in his notes, and I must decide between the two."

Her lips parted as her jaw dropped slightly. He had to agree with her expression. It was a foolish thing to be avoiding.

"Would you like help?" she asked.

"You would lend me your artist's eye?"

"I do not –" she stopped, pressed her lips together, and drew a breath. "Yes. If you will show me the room to be painted and tell me the colours from which you need to choose, I will give you my opinion."

He held his arm out to her. She gave it a cautious look but then, placed her hand on it ever so lightly as if she was not sure if she should. Yes, he had made a fabulous impression on Miss Bennet. Hopefully, it was not such a poor impression that she refused to visit Maggie and Rose ever again, for he was certain neither of them would forgive him if he had chased their special friend away.

Chapter 6

"Would you like to go through the music room or the library?" Mr. Alford asked as he and Mary passed beneath the arch at the end of the long gallery.

Her eyes swept the anteroom. There were more paintings here. She would dearly like to know who each of these people was, but she would not ask. She would just have to content herself with the knowledge that they were probably relations.

To her left was a smaller hall, while to her right was another stairway. It was not so large and ornate as the one she had taken earlier, but it was by no means lacking in elegant details. Every inch of this house held something she could study for hours.

"The family stairs," Mr. Alford said. "And these portraits are of my grandparents and great grandparents."

It was as if he knew what questions she was thinking. He was very unsettling. And not just because he was handsome and smelled lovely – like cedar and lemons.

"The music room is to our left and the library to our right. Which will it be?"

She wanted to see both rooms, but since she had to pick one... "The library?"

He chuckled. "What if we enter through the library and exit through the music room? How does that sound?"

"That sounds like a perfect plan." It was still unsettling that he seemed to know her thoughts, but in this case, she was grateful that it would satisfy her curiosity.

He opened the door on the right side of the anteroom just beyond the family stairs.

"You, there," he called to a maid who was scurrying towards a door at one end of the library that Mary assumed led to a servant's staircase.

"Yes, sir," the young girl said with a curtsey. "How may I be of service?"

"Could you pretend to dust something here in the library and then in the music room if it is required?"

"Pretend, sir?" The maid, whom Mary recognized as the one who had helped her earlier, looked utterly astonished by such a request. She supposed it was not often that a servant was asked to pretend her chores by her employer.

Mr. Alford nodded as he said, "I assume you have already done your duty since you were just leaving, so I doubt there will be anything left to clean. However, I would like to keep things proper for Miss Bennet."

Oh! Mary had not thought of that. Her own maid was likely waiting for the carriage – or in the carriage – by now. She was incredibly grateful that Mr. Alford had thought about her reputation when she, herself, had not given it a second's thought.

"Of course, sir," the maid replied.

"Thank you..." He seemed lost for a name.

"Martha," Mary whispered.

"Martha?" he said in surprise.

"Yes, that is my name," the maid said with a smile for Mary.

"But how did you know that?" he asked Mary.

"She helped me find the right door to the nursery earlier. I told Mr. Branston that I remembered the way, but as it turns out, I did not. There are several turns in that hallway."

"There are, indeed," he agreed. He seemed to be pondering something unpleasant as she watched his brow furrow and his eyes lose their sparkle. "I must admit." His eyes met hers. "I am a little ashamed that you know my servants' names and I do not. I usually know everyone in my place of residence, unless it is an inn."

"You have just arrived home," Mary hurried to assure him. She had not meant to cause him discomfort. She had only wanted to help him. Why was it that she seemed unable to remember how to be a proper lady and say the proper things when she was speaking to him? "I am certain that Martha cannot be the only staff member who is new since you were last here."

"That is true." He looked somewhat mollified.

"And I only know the servants to whom I have been introduced. I dare say you know far more of them than I do."

"That is also true." He smiled at her, and she wanted to sigh. He was a beautiful man both in features and character, for a man of ugly character would not care if he knew his servants' names.

"And here we are," he said. "This is the room that, according to Broderick's schedule, is next to be refreshed."

"This room is lovely!" Mary cried as she and Mr. Alford passed through a door in the left-hand corner of the library to a small drawing room that was attached to the library.

"Just this room?" Mr. Alford chuckled. "What about the library?" His tone was teasing. "Most people who enter that room have some comment to make about it, but you did not."

Mary removed her hand from his arm and, turning, went back to the library. "I must admit I was too caught up in our conversation to take it in." How was she supposed to remember to look at a room when she was looking at a handsome gentleman?

"And now that we are no longer discussing my servants, what do you think of the library?"

"It has a great number of books."

"That is why we call it a library," he whispered near her ear.

"I know that," she retorted and brushed at her ear to try to remove the tingling sensation his breath had caused. "But not all libraries have this many books. Pemberley's does, of course. Mr. Darcy is a great reader and likes to be surrounded by knowledge. However, Netherfield's library is sparse, and unless Jane wishes to see it improved, it will remain sparse, although I do not expect Jane will stay at Netherfield long enough to see a library filled."

"Netherfield?"

"It is the estate next to my father's and where my sister Jane and her husband, Mr. Bingley, live. Mr. Bingley is not a great reader. He is more of a talker. He makes a wonderful conversationalist at any event he attends." It was quite easy to like Mr. Bingley. He was amongst the most amiable people Mary had ever met.

"Ah, yes. I think I have met Mr. Bingley years ago. He is a good friend of Mr. Darcy, is he not?"

"They are the best of friends, and now they are brothers. The colours in here are very somber. That seems fitting. And the furniture does not proclaim itself. That is also fitting to the purpose of the room."

"Is it?" he asked with some interest.

"Most certainly. A library's focus should be the knowledge it contains, not the décor. However, do not tell my mother I said so. She would think I was very strange to want to see a book displayed rather than a tufted footstool."

He took a few steps into his library and turned a circle as if seeing the room for the first time. "I might have to agree with your mother," he said as he turned. "Not that it is strange to display books more prominently in a room designed for them than to display the furniture – though I will admit that I had never truly considered that fact before," he stopped his perusal of the room and looked directly at her. "However, I must say that it does make me think you are unusual."

Was he calling her odd?

His lips quirked up on the right side as if he knew what she was thinking – again! Insufferable man! She turned back to the music room.

"I do not believe I have ever met a lady who would value knowledge above fashion," he said as he joined her. "I am happy to say I now have."

She shot him a questioning look.

"Unusual is not bad," he said softly. "Is it not just another word for rare?"

"I am not sure I like that term any better," she muttered.

"There is almost always a higher price attached to anything bearing the mark *rare*." He folded his arms across his chest and arched one eyebrow as if challenging her to disagree with him.

She could not help smiling at both his words and his expression. "Thank you."

He bowed his head in acceptance. "You are most welcome, Miss Bennet." He motioned back towards the library. "Are you a great reader?"

"I would not say so."

His expression was doubtful. "Is this similar to how you think you do not have an artistic eye?"

She laughed. "Perhaps. I enjoy reading very much. However, the sorts of books I enjoy reading are not broad. A library to house the sorts of books I like to read would not need to be overly big at all."

"Novels?" he whispered as if it was a dreadful secret.

Again, she laughed. "No. I prefer books on the improvement of one's self."

A confused crease formed between his eyebrows. "Do you mean you enjoy books of manners?"

"Yes, but not just books of manners. There is extraordinarily little need to know how to appear on the outside if the inside is full of dust and debris. That would be much like painting the door to a home and securing it with the largest and most secure lock while ignoring the fact that there are holes in the ceiling, and the windows have no glass or shutters."

He still looked perplexed. "You will have to tell me what books you consider to be secure windows and solid roof tiles."

"Sermons and scripture." She held his gaze, waiting to see the revulsion she usually saw in someone's eyes when she admitted to enjoying such reading material. They all assumed it was because she thought she was better than they were. But she knew she was not. In fact, that is why she read them – to remind herself of her need to improve and to help guide herself along in doing so. It was not as if she had a mother to whom she could turn to ask deep questions, her father would likely tease her before he answered her question, and neither of them would understand her need to question their answers. But so often, the answers to one question begat more questions, and one must not simply accept a truth as true without giving it a good bit of thought.

Mr. Alford's eyes grew wide, and he blinked. Her answer had obviously startled him, but he was not seeking the closest exit. Instead, he did something rather startling by grabbing her hand and leading her back to the library where he pulled her halfway down its length on the left side to a set of shelves that stood between two windows.

"We call this the Aaron Collection," he said with a wave of his hand – the one that was not still holding hers and causing her fingers to tingle in a most enjoyable fashion. "I think you will find many tomes here that would interest you."

He was not trying to escape but rather providing her with a place to find books that she enjoyed as if it was something he was proud to do? How unusual. Her lips curled up in a smile. Or she should say, how rare.

"I have read many of them myself," Mr. Alford said, "although I must admit it was only because Aaron asked me to do so. He wanted someone to question him on the contents."

Mary's free hand flew to her heart. "He *wanted* someone to question him?"

"Yes! He said it was the best way to be certain he understood the material." He shrugged. "Is that not what a professor does when examining his scholars?"

"I suppose it is, though I have never been to school; therefore, I am just choosing to believe what you say is true since you have been to school."

He shook his head. "You may not have been to an academic institution, but you have been to school."

"I assure you that I have not."

He led her back toward the drawing room. "Do you play the piano?"

"Yes, though some would say I do not do it well."

"And how would they know?"

She looked at him in surprise. That seemed a most absurd question.

"You have performed," he answered for her. "You learned the notes and their patterns, and then, the good professor, Dr. Performance, examined your learning."

She shook her head. "That is ridiculous."

"But true," he pressed. "Do you sew?"

"Of course."

"Just needlework or clothing?"

"Both."

"Did you make this dress?"

"No, it used to be Elizabeth's."

"But you made it yours in some way, did you not? I have heard too many females chattering about embellishments to believe you did not alter this dress in some fashion. Was it the addition of lace or a sash?" He had released her hand finally, but only so he could capture the ribbon that she had added to this gown because she thought it brightened it.

"Both that ribbon and this lace," she touched the lace at her neckline.

He glanced at the lace before finding her eyes with his own. She could not read the expression in his eyes, but the atmosphere of the room seemed to have shifted.

"They both seem to be securely attached and not soon to fall off." He looked at the ribbon he held and then dropped it, pulling his hand back quickly as if the ribbon was a hot tong.

"My point is," he said, turning from her to look at the room, "we learn, and our learning is tested – questioned, if you will. If I read about a new method of crop management and agree that it is better than an old method, then when I put it into practice my knowledge is questioned by nature. Sometimes, I succeed on the first attempt. Other times, I have to make adjustments and refine my learning. I might even have to reread what I first read." He turned his head to look at her. "You may be unschooled, Miss Bennet, but you are not unlearned. Never think you are."

His sincerity warmed her heart. "That sounds very much like something your brother would say. You must have learned well when questioning him."

He smiled, but it was not an expression of delight. Rather, it looked rueful, and there was a shadow of sadness that crossed his features. "And through the trials of life."

"From which colours do you have to choose?" It felt safest to change the subject back to what it should be even if Mary would rather talk to him about what trials he had faced that helped him learn about the things he had read.

"The note on the list said green or red."

"Red? In this room?" Oh, no! That would not do.

"You do not like that idea? The word cozy was next to the word red."

"Do you see how the light from that one small window fills this room?"

He nodded.

"If the walls were red, they would steal some of that light. This room would feel cozy and snug – I will give you that. However, I think it would also feel dark. How do you use this room?"

"I don't."

She caught herself just before she rolled her eyes at his reply. Of course, he had not used it in years and maybe never did when he lived here as a young man. However, it was his home now, and he might eventually use it.

"Then tell me how you would wish for it to be used?"

He shrugged. "I do not know. It is a passage between the music room and the library."

"Is that its only purpose?"

He looked at her as if bewildered. "How would you use it?"

She took a moment to ponder that. "With a chair, such as this one," she walked over to a chair that had wings on it, which would be perfect for resting one's head against when weary, "placed near the window, this room could be a fabulous place to do some stitching or reading in the afternoon when it is not cloudy." She turned and went to the desk along the wall near the door that she assumed went to the music room. "Or move this desk into the corner and with a lamp on it or a sconce on the wall, this room could be a lovely, quiet place to do some writing."

"Or sketching?" he added.

"Yes, or sketching." A thought grasped her, causing her to clap her hands as she warmed to the idea of using this room. "Tea with friends in this room would also be perfectly wonderful since it is snug compared to the other reception rooms I have seen. Oh! Or after dinner, the ladies could retire here – a card table would be just the right size in here, I should think – and their husbands could hold discussions in the library if they were so inclined before an interlude of music was enjoyed to complete the night."

He was smiling broadly. "You paint a very pretty domestic picture. This room has never been used very much, but then, perhaps that is because no one saw its potential as you have described it."

A sense of pride swelled within her. He approved of her ideas. *Her* ideas.

"And you would paint it green?" he asked.

"May I peek at the colours in the music room before I commit to the choice?"

He blinked. "Of course."

She looked through the door he opened into a large and rather open room. There was a piano at one side and a harp in the corner. A seating area was positioned near a hearth, and a few other chairs and pieces of furniture stood here and there. With very little effort, the furniture could be pushed back, and the carpet rolled up to make room for a dance. If a group of neighbors could dance in the drawing room at Lucas Lodge which was not as grand as this, they could most certainly dance here. However, that was not what she was supposed to be evaluating.

"Are you repainting this room?"

"Not this year. I understand it was refreshed just three years ago, before Sarah died."

"I assume Sarah was your brother's wife?"

His jaw clenched as if he was uncomfortable with her question. "She was."

"I apologize. I did not mean to bring up your brother."

He shook his head. "It is not that." His shoulders

lifted and lowered as he took a breath. "Shall I paint the drawing room green?"

"I believe it would be an excellent choice. A light sage would be lovely and would blend this lighter creamy yellow with the darker wood panels of the library. I think it would be a wonderful transition." She touched his arm to draw his attention. "Do you see the rug in here?"

"Yes."

"What is its dominant colour?"

"Crimson."

"And what other colours do you see?"

He shook his head as if he did not understand why she would ask such an obvious question. "Blue, yellow, gold..." He paused and a smile tipped his lips. "Green."

"You will want something in that shade but not as dark. If I remember correctly, there is at least one chair in the library which is green."

"I would have never thought to tie the rooms together."

"And yet, you described this drawing room as having no other purpose." She held his gaze.

"I suppose I did." He extended his arm to her.

"Do you wish to see more of the music room? I could have Martha dust a table."

Mary chuckled as she placed her hand on his arm. "No, I am quite certain Mr. Branston will be sending out a search party for me soon since my carriage and my maid are probably both waiting impatiently for me on the drive." She would rather stay here. However, she was expected back at Pemberley at a particular time, and she did not wish to risk running afoul of Mr. Darcy and not being allowed to return to Wellworth Abbey with just a maid as a chaperone.

"Will you allow me to escort you to the door so I can explain your delay?"

"It is not necessary." She would, however, like that very much. "I am sure you have many things that need your attention."

He held up a finger as if placing a bookmark in the middle of their conversation and turned to Martha. "Thank you, Martha. Your imaginary dusting skills are as brilliant as your real ones. You may return to your other duties. I do hope I did not delay you too greatly."

"It was my pleasure, sir." She dipped a curtsey. "Miss Bennet." She dipped another curtsey and then stood at the servants' door until Mary and Mr. Alford had exited the library.

"I did not ask you, Miss Bennet, if it was necessary for me to escort you to the door. I am almost positive you can find it without my assistance." There was a slight teasing twinge to his tone. It was a much more pleasant sort of teasing than what she endured at home from her father and sisters.

"Are you saying you *want* to escort me to the door?" She asked as they strolled down the long gallery toward the grand staircase and the table on which she had discarded her sketching supplies.

"That is precisely what I am saying, Miss Bennet."

She glanced at him – a handsome man who valued both her and her ideas and did not want to be quickly rid of her. It was a most delightful feeling. "Then, Mr. Alford, I would be happy to allow you the pleasure."

Chapter 7

"Did you come to see me?" Aaron asked with a laugh when Stuart jumped down from his carriage and turned to lift Maggie out.

"Yes," Stuart replied while Maggie said a joyful *no*, and Rose shook her head.

"Well, at least one of you has come to visit me."

"We will visit you, too," Maggie assured Aaron.

"But you came to see Miss Bennet, did you not?" Aaron asked.

"We did." Stuart held out his hands to Rose. She gave them a cautious look but then, stepped forward so she could be lifted out of the vehicle. "Miss Bennet said two days ago that she was nearly finished with her sketch of your home, so we thought that perhaps today, with it being such a lovely, warm day, she might be here."

"And she is," Aaron said. "I was just going out to visit with the ladies for a bit before they leave."

"Hurry." Maggie pulled on Stuart's hand. Panic laced her voice.

"She will not leave without seeing you." Both Miss Bennet and Miss Darcy had waved a greeting to the carriage as it passed close to where they were seated.

"But I want to see her now." Maggie's pout was just about visible, though she appeared to be working to look pleasant and not disgruntled. Miss Leslie had said that it was not unusual for a child to pout when he or she did not get his or her way, but she assured Stuart that she had been working with Maggie on not pouting, since such a habit was not acceptable for a young lady who wished to be thought of as an enjoyable friend.

"Patience," Miss Leslie whispered.

Maggie's features fell to disappointment, but the tugging on Stuart's hand ceased. Patience was not an easy virtue to master at any age. If Stuart were to be honest, he was looking forward to seeing Miss Bennet himself. He had quite enjoyed his talk with her when she was at Wellworth Abbey.

"You may walk ahead of us with Rose," Stuart offered.

"But do not run," Miss Leslie added as she followed quickly behind the two young Miss Alfords.

"You seem to be doing well with them," Aaron commented when the girls and Miss Leslie were a short distance ahead of them.

"It is not quite as hard as I expected it to be, but I will not lie and say it is easy. I do not know how anyone goes from bachelor to father with ease."

"They usually begin with marriage and have several months to adjust to the idea of being a father to just one infant at a time. Rarely do they have two youngsters thrust upon them with little notice."

"I suppose that is true, but it does seem that someone who has had siblings should be able to adjust to the idea of being the guardian of two children more easily than it seems to fall to me. I think Miss Leslie may need her salary increased since it seems she has taken on an additional pupil. I have little idea how to help a young girl become a young lady."

"I would be shocked if anyone with only brothers would know that. Indeed, I have met plenty of gentlemen with sisters who still have little idea what it takes to mould a young girl into a proper young lady."

Aaron's hands were clasped behind his back as he walked at a sedate pace towards where Miss Bennet and Miss Darcy were seated. He glanced warily at Stuart.

"Just say it." Stuart knew that look. Aaron was thinking something that he thought needed to be said but was something which might make Stuart angry.

"A wife might make your job easier."

"I am sure you are correct, which is why Broderick should have left the girls to you."

"I have no wife."

"No, but you also have no aversion to taking one."

Aaron huffed. "Are you going to allow Sarah to steal all your happiness?"

"It was not Sarah who did the stealing."

"Yes, it was." Aaron took hold of Stuart's arm and stopped him. "Broderick was not without fault, but the greatest share of the blame must fall to the schemer who played brother against brother to gain all she wanted."

Stuart's brow furrowed. "What do you mean?"

"I cannot say. Not yet." Aaron moved to continue walking, but Stuart prevented him.

"Explain yourself."

Aaron pressed his lips together and shook his head. "Do you still love her?"

Stuart blinked. That was an unexpected shift in the conversation. "Sarah?"

"Yes."

"I am not certain how I feel about her at present," Stuart answered with a half-hearted shrug. "But I can say that I do not hate her as I did. Indeed, I discovered just the other day that I felt truly little when I saw her portrait. There was some bitterness, some sadness, and a flash of anger." He shrugged again. "Of course, it was all mixed with the knowledge of how utterly stupid I was."

"You were not stupid. You were duped. It happens to many good people."

"No. Not to me – and not by someone so dear."

"You are not so special that you cannot be tricked," his brother protested.

"That is not what I meant." Although as Stuart gave a moment's thought to what his words could have meant other than he was too intelligent to be deceived, he could not think of any other way to explain them.

"You must take what I am about to tell you to your grave." Aaron's expression was more serious than Stuart had ever seen it. "Sarah's cousin duped Darcy."

What was his brother talking about? Sarah only had one cousin – a fellow named George Wickham. How had Wickham duped Darcy? Darcy knew what sort of scoundrel Wickham was. Everyone in their circle of acquaintances knew that Wickham was not to be trusted.

"Wickham?" he asked just to be certain he was thinking about the correct scoundrel.

"You and I both know how cautious Darcy can be," Aaron continued.

Stuart shook his head, trying to clear it enough to accept the idea that Darcy could be fooled by a man like Wickham.

"However, Wickham arranged things so that he could charm Darcy's sister." Aaron's voice was barely above a whisper.

Stuart turned to look at Miss Darcy. "She is not even out yet." Apparently, Wickham was even worse than Stuart had heard he was. Who preyed on a schoolgirl?

"I know, and so did Wickham. He did not work alone. He had an accomplice. Do you remember Mrs. Younge?"

Dread filled Stuart's heart at the mention of the name. "The same Mrs. Younge who was Sarah's companion during her first season in town?" Sarah had been very fond of Mrs. Younge and had sung her praises to Stuart on many occasions.

Aaron nodded.

"Darcy hired her for his sister. As it turns out, Mrs. Younge is a good friend of Wickham. Indeed, it was through Sarah that Wickham came to know Mrs. Younge. And, now you know why Sarah found it so easy to sneak out to meet you." Aaron leaned a little close to his brother. "She had no need to sneak. Mrs. Younge will turn a blind eye for a tuppence."

"Is Miss Darcy –" He wanted to know the extent of the damage Wickham had done, but he also knew it was not his business to know that much detail. "Is she well?"

"Does she seem well to you?"

"She does, but I have not seen her in years so I would not know if there were a change, would I?"

Aaron chuckled. "I suppose you would not. She seems to be recovering well. Mrs. Annesley has been a great help to her." He leaned close to Stuart once again. "She is not ruined, and last I heard, Wickham was bound for Ireland at the insistence of Colonel Fitzwilliam."

"Her cousin?"

"Yes. Something happened at Christmas time. I do not know the details, and if I did, I would not be free to share them with you."

"And yet, you have already shared several details that I would imagine neither Miss Darcy nor Mr. Darcy would wish to have shared."

"Nor would their cousin." Aaron gave Stuart a pointed look. "That is why you will take this to your grave."

"Or run the risk of being sent to my grave on a field of honour?"

"You do know the colonel."

"I do. I heard he has married."

"He is. To Miss Bingley. Do you remember her?"

Stuart's brow furrowed as he searched his memories of the few times he had been in company with

Darcy and his friend Mr. Bingley. "I believe I do. She is a pretty, sharp-tongued lady, if I am remembering correctly, and a little above herself."

"She *was*. Miss Darcy assures me that she has found a softer side, thanks to Colonel Fitzwilliam."

Aaron's lips tipped up on one side. Apparently, some serendipitous thought had struck him, for the expression he wore was one he had often worn when something had come into focus for him when they were young.

"Is that not what one spouse should do for another?" Aaron asked. "Should they not encourage and draw out the best in the person they love?"

"I have always thought so, and you know Father always said so."

"But emotions are tricky, and desires can cloud what is and what is not."

Did parsons take a course at university on how to purposefully state things in ways that would necessitate their expounding on them to make them clear? Mr. Moore had been excellent at offering Stuart hidden bits of wisdom when Stuart had first arrived in Devon with his heart in tatters.

"Ask yourself if Sarah drew out the best in you and if you ever once considered how you could be her complement. Maybe that will help you sort out how you view her now."

Yes, it must be part of their training. Would it not just be easier for Aaron to tell him what he needed to know? Stuart scowled.

"I could answer this for you, of course, but we both know you will learn more from coming to your own conclusion than you will from your little brother sharing his opinion with you."

"I am not sure you are correct about that."

Aaron laughed. "Yes, you are. You just do not want to admit that I am right."

Stuart shrugged. "That could be true." He did know that Aaron was correct.

"Bring your answer to me when you have it, and we can see if we agree." He waved a hand towards Miss Bennet as if to say to move forward.

"You are not going to explain yourself, are you?"

"About Sarah playing brother against brother?"

"Yes."

"No, I am not." And with that, he trotted the remaining distance to where Miss Bennet was attempting to sketch with one young girl sitting close to each of her arms.

She certainly must have heaps of patience to be

able to continue drawing while entertaining Maggie and Rose. Those two were not the sort to just sit quietly by and watch – or he should say Maggie was not. Rose, on the other hand, was seemingly content to be quiet and thoughtful for long stretches of time.

"And at my home," Miss Bennet was saying as he drew close enough to hear the conversation, "there was a swing on the tree between the house and the barn. It was a favourite place for us to play when we were little, and a wonderful place to sit and think as we got older."

"Did all your sisters swing on it?" Maggie asked.

"We did."

"Did your Papa put it up for you?"

"No, he had someone do it for him."

"Did he ever come to see you swing on it?"

Mary shook her head. "Not me."

Her eyes lifted from her work to greet Stuart as he approached her. There was something very matter of fact and yet sad about how she had replied.

"But he came to see your sisters?" he asked before she could even welcome him.

Her smile faltered before becoming something that seemed forced. That was interesting.

"Not all of them."

His head tilted as he contemplated her response. He wanted to ask more, but he knew he had already been too forward. To his curiosity's delight, she supplied a bit more information. Bless her!

"Elizabeth and my father have a special bond."

"Elizabeth?" Stuart asked. "She is Mrs. Darcy now, is she not?"

"Yes."

"I would imagine your father must miss her."

"He does." She chuckled softly. "He bemoans the fact that he no longer has a sensible daughter at home." He must not have hidden his surprise at such a comment very well, for she hastened to add, "He is mostly teasing. It is not that none of the rest of us are not sensible. We are just not Elizabeth."

There was that hint of sadness again.

"What are your other sisters called?" Rose asked.

"She told us that," Maggie scolded.

"There are a lot of us, it is not hard to forget the names." Miss Bennet lowered her voice and whispered as if sharing the most delicious secret,

"Sometimes, my mother says the wrong name when calling to us."

Maggie and Rose giggled.

"I do not think I have ever heard the names of your sisters," Aaron said.

"I have, though it was only in passing," Stuart said. "Let me see if I can remember. There is Elizabeth who is Mrs. Darcy. Then, there is Jane, who is Mrs. Bingley." He stopped. "Is Elizabeth or Jane older?"

"Jane," Miss Bennet replied with a smile. "Then, it is Elizabeth and then me."

"Thank you. I will do my best to remember the order for next time."

"There are more," Rose said.

The fact that she had been the one to prompt him was a delight. She was slowly warming up to him. Perhaps before the summer was out, he would be given the pleasure of reading to her in the reading chair or receiving a hug at the end of breakfast. For now, he would just be content to receive this little nod of approval.

"I know. I think there are only two more, unless, of course, Miss Bennet has not mentioned a sister when speaking to me." He shot a questioning glance at Miss Bennet who merely shrugged and tucked her lips in as if to say she was not telling. It was enjoyable to see the very proper-looking Miss Bennet be slightly playful. "There is Kitty who is betrothed to someone, but I do not know who, and she likes to write stories, and then, I think the youngest is Lydia because she was mentioned as being young and lively. How did I do?"

"Exceptionally well," Miss Bennet replied. "Kitty is marrying Mr. Linton, and Lydia is the youngest."

"There are no secret sisters?"

Miss Bennet shook her head but then gasped. "There is Miss Darcy. She is a new sister."

"As are Mr. Bingley's sisters and Mr. Linton's sister, when Kitty marries," Miss Darcy added.

"That is a lot of sisters," Aaron said with a laugh.

"And I now have nearly the same number of brothers," Mary said with a smile. "And to think I started life with no brothers at all."

"I would like a brother," Maggie said sadly. "Papa said brothers were fun." She sighed. "Our brother died with Mama."

"Oh!" Miss Bennet cried, dropping her pencil and wrapping an arm around Maggie and Rose. "I had forgotten that. I should have been more care-ful." Her eyes begged Stuart to pardon her.

"How did you know?" Maggie asked.

"Your uncle told me when I saw the portrait of your mother and father. Remember how Miss Leslie told me about the long gallery?"

Maggie nodded.

"Your uncle was there."

"Was he?"

Stuart did not like the tone or expression that accompanied Aaron's comment.

"He was," Stuart answered. "I was on my way to pick a colour to paint the drawing room between the library and music room."

"Ah," Aaron said.

It still did not look as if his brother's interest was appeased.

"We came to the decision that a light sage would be best."

Aaron's eyebrows flew towards his hairline. "You did?" He looked from Stuart to Miss Bennet and back.

"We did, and Martha did not seem to disap-prove, so I think it was the correct decision."

"Martha?"

"Do you not know the maids at Wellworth?" he teased his brother.

"Not all of them."

"Well, then, when you come around next, I will have to introduce you to her." He turned to Miss Bennet. "Speaking of the drawing room. The painters will begin their work next week. When it is complete, you will have to come see if it looks as you imagined it."

"I would like that." Her gaze dropped from his as she picked up her pencil.

Was she blushing because she thought it was more than just a friendly invitation? He hoped not, for it wasn't. At least, he was nearly certain that he had only invited her to thank her for her help and not simply because he rather liked talking to her and, therefore, wished to see her again.

Chapter 8

Mary walked into church two days later with her shoulders lifted, her head held high, and her heart buoyed with gratitude. She was certain she had never smiled as much as she had since last seeing Mr. Alford and his nieces. Not only had both Maggie and Rose been anxious to see her, but their uncle had also thought well enough of her advice in choosing a paint colour that he had invited her to visit.

It was an excellent sign that her stay in Derbyshire might just prove to be as wonderful as she had hoped it would be because perhaps there were others here who, like Mr. Alford, might also see her for herself and not merely as someone's sister. After all, Mr. Alford knew all her sisters' names and had even met Elizabeth and still, he acknowledged Mary for herself. It was a most delicious feeling and so different from how she was seen in Meryton.

Her eyes settled on the back of Elizabeth's bonnet. Had her sisters always known this feeling of having one's opinions valued? The idea caused a moment of jealousy to prick her heart. She could not speak for Jane, Elizabeth, or Kitty – though she strongly suspected Lizzy and Jane had never felt the sting of censure the way she had – but she knew for a fact that Lydia most certainly must have known how it was to have her opinion valued, for she seemed to think everyone thought she was the best at everything. Mary's lips twitched as she considered the fact that if someone did not acknowledge Lydia as the best, she would simply decide that they were not worth knowing.

This feeling of being accomplished must be carefully carried. Mary had no desire to wear her pride as Lydia did. For now, however, she would allow herself the indulgence of feeling her worth as seen by another.

The handsome gentleman who was the cause of Mary's current effervescent mood was seated just two rows behind where Mr. Darcy motioned for her and Georgiana to follow Aunt and Uncle Gardiner into a pew and take a seat. Before sitting down, Mary turned and gave a small nod of her head to Maggie and Rose, who had very carefully waved at her. She had to admit that Mr. Alford and his nieces made a lovely family picture. Miss Leslie sat next to Rose at the end of the pew, and Maggie sat next to her uncle with her hand tucked into his. It was a most arresting sight, that one small black-gloved hand resting beneath a larger one. Such faith, such trust was in that small action. Perhaps she would attempt to draw it later. It would be a fabulous reminder of how she was to trust God.

Mr. Alford smiled at her and gave an almost imperceivable nod of welcome. It was enough to startle Mary from her contemplations. Quickly, she sat down. Her cheeks were surely red for they felt quite warm. She cast a sidelong glance at Georgiana. Her new sister and friend looked thoroughly amused.

"I was just greeting Maggie," Mary whispered.

"I am certain you were." There was a hint of a laugh in Georgiana's tone that said she did not believe Mary.

"I do not like him like that," Mary hissed. Not that she was incapable of liking him like as one would a suitor. She just knew that she was not the sort of lady someone, who was as handsome as Mr. Alford, married. She had seen the portrait of his brother's wife. Maggie's mother was a beauty. Mary was not, and she was certain that her ability to pick paint colours and draw sketches of chairs recommended her to him for nothing more than the position of a person hired to oversee a restoration project.

"So you say," Georgiana replied.

Mary was learning that new sisters could be just as teasing as old sisters. There had been more than one comment made on the way home to Pemberley, after drawing at the parsonage the other day, about how kind it was of Mr. Alford to invite Mary to his home, and another comment or two had been made about Mary's time alone with him in the library. Thankfully, Georgiana had been good enough not to tease Mary about any of that in front of Elizabeth, Mr. Darcy, or Aunt and Uncle Gardiner.

Aunt Gardiner leaned toward her and whispered, "He is handsome."

Mary closed her eyes. "I was greeting Maggie," she whispered.

"It would not be a bad thing to be greeting their uncle," her aunt replied. "He seemed happy to see you."

"It would be very strange if he scowled at me," Mary retorted. "He was being polite."

Aunt Gardiner chuckled but said no more.

"Maybe he was happy to see you," Georgiana whispered just before the service began. "And maybe he was glad to see that you were happy to see him."

"You do not think..." Mary could not put her full thought into words. It was too humiliating. She was not a flirt!

Georgiana only shrugged in response.

For that next hour and fifteen minutes, Mary performed as she was expected to when in church, but her mind was not on the music, scripture, or sermon. It was occupied with worrying about appearing to be forward. Mr. Alford would never want her to visit Wellworth to call on Maggie and Rose if he thought she was only doing it to gain his attention. That was something Lydia would do, which in Mary's mind put it firmly on the improper list of ways to gain the notice of a gentleman. Not that she was trying to gain Mr. Alford's notice. She wasn't.

The more she thought about how things might appear to Mr. Alford, the more she had to work at keeping both her shoulders and head lifted. Her heart could not be kept from sinking. She was still thankful that Mr. Alford had valued her opinion on something, but she could not feel as light as she had. The thought of being seen as no more than a flirt by Mr. Alford was a painful thing, and that was worrying because it meant she valued his opinion more than she should.

"You appear confused," her aunt whispered as the final prayer concluded.

"I am merely contemplating things," Mary replied before following Mr. Darcy and Elizabeth out of their pew and down the aisle of the church. She walked as quickly as she could so that her aunt could not question her further. She had no desire to discuss her contemplations with anyone. Indeed, she wished that she did not even have to think about them herself.

"Miss Bennet," Mr. Aaron Alford called as she crossed through the door of the nave to the churchyard.

Mary turned toward him, but he motioned her forward and walked with her. It really would not do to cause a blockade at the door to the church.

"I just wanted to thank you for the drawing," he said. "I had no idea you were making a copy for me."

"You were so kind to let me draw your charming home. It was the least I could do to thank you. I am happy to hear it was delivered without issue."

"I plan to hang it in my study. Your work is most excellent."

"Thank you." If her mind was not so troubled with thoughts of flirting and longing to be valued by the parson's brother, Mary might have felt the compliment of his words even more than she currently did. However, her mind, and therefore, her enjoyment, were muddled with awkwardness.

"You and Miss Darcy will not be strangers now that your drawing is finished, will you be?" He glanced hopefully at Miss Darcy. There was no mistaking that his invitation to Mary was for the purpose of seeing Georgiana again.

"You will have to ask Mr. Darcy, I should think," Mary replied. "However, I am certain I am not opposed to visiting. Are you, Georgiana?"

"No, not at all," Georgiana answered.

Mary cocked a questioning brow at her friend as if to say, "Is that so?" Georgiana's eyes grew wide at the taunt that lay behind the expression. If Georgiana was going to tease Mary about Mr. Stuart Alford, then it seemed only fair that Mary should be able to tease her about Mr. Aaron Alford.

"I will ask your brother then, Miss Darcy. I would be quite delighted to have him and his wife visit with you, and your aunt and uncle as well, Miss Bennet. I am a social sort of person." He laughed lightly. "Allow me to go greet a few others. It was good to see you this morning. I hope you enjoyed the sermon."

"I found much to consider." Mary's cheeks were once again feeling warm. It was not a complete lie. She had found a great deal to think about during the sermon. Of course, none of those things actually had anything to do with the sermon, so in reality, it was nothing more than a lie coated with a thin varnish of truth to make it palatable. She sighed.

"Honestly," she said before he could dart away, "I found my mind wandering, but it was not of your doing nor did it have anything to do with your ability to give a sermon."

"Indeed?"

She nodded. "I apologize for trying to make it sound like I was contemplating the sermon when I was not."

He chuckled. "You are forgiven, and may I applaud you for being one of the few who will admit that they were not paying attention. It speaks to a good heart."

"My heart is not good, sir."

His eyebrows flew upward.

"If it were, I would not have attempted to deceive you, and I am sure I would have paid closer attention to your sermon."

His head cocked to the side. "Am I to gather that you hold truth in high esteem?" He seemed somewhat amused but not in a mocking way. In fact, he appeared to be somewhat pleased.

"I do, though it is not always easy to be as honest as one should be."

He smiled. "I would agree with that, but I may have to disagree with your not having a good heart."

"But the scripture says –"

He held up a finger, as if a thought had just occurred to him, cutting off her rebuttal. "Perhaps I should rephrase it from you have a good heart to you have a heart that desires good."

"That, I could accept," Mary replied.

"Are you and Miss Bennet disagreeing again?" Mr. Stuart Alford asked as he joined his brother.

"We were, but we have just now reached a mutually agreeable compromise. Indeed, I think the compromise is better than my original thought." He bowed to Mary. "I will have to ponder it this afternoon as I drive to Wellworth Abbey."

"I was just going to remind you of your obligation to visit with us," Mr. Stuart Alford said. "Maggie was afraid you would forget."

"I could never forget an obligation to my nieces or my brother."

"That is what I told her, but she insisted."

"I will be there at the expected time. Give her and Rose a kiss for me." And with that and a final bow to the ladies, he was off to talk to other parishioners.

"Did you enjoy the sermon?"

Mary sighed while Georgiana giggled.

"Did I say something humorous?" Mr. Alford asked.

"No, it is just the same question your brother asked that caused our disagreement," Mary replied. "I am certain the sermon was excellent. The few bits and pieces that made their way into my mind seemed to be. However, I must admit, much to my shame, that I was not attending to it as I should have been. My thoughts were elsewhere."

Mr. Alford's brow furrowed for a moment before he extended one arm to Mary and another to Georgiana. "Allow me to see you to Mr. Darcy's carriage."

"Thank you. That is kind."

"Was there anything in particular about which you were thinking?"

Mary closed her eyes and shook her head. Of all the things to be asked at a moment when honesty was foremost in her mind.

"Yes," she answered and then added, "I must admit that both Maggie and Rose were exceptionally quiet during the service. My youngest sisters were not always so obliging when they were young." Lydia was still not as quiet as she likely should be.

"Rose fell asleep," Mr. Alford said. "And Maggie was content to simply play with my fingers and rest her head against my shoulder."

"That is lovely," Georgiana said.

"It is," Mary agreed.

"I doubt either one of them were actually listening to the sermon, however."

"Which is not unusual for a young child," Mary assured him. "Sermons are not light subjects and take a great deal of thinking to appreciate them properly, would you not agree?"

"Indeed, I would. And if one's mind is otherwise engaged, it does make it challenging to enjoy a sermon as one might wish to do, would you not agree?"

Was he attempting to discover what she had been thinking about instead of listening to the parson? Well, she was not about to admit to that easily. "I would agree."

"You are not going to tell me what thoughts were distracting you, are you?" he asked with a soft chuckle that seemed to sound a trifle tense.

"No. I would prefer to keep that to myself. It is shameful enough to admit that I was not doing as I was supposed to be doing."

"Some might say shameful. Others might say normal."

"I am not others, Mr. Alford. I know what is right and proper, and I strive to do it as best I can. I feel it most profoundly when I fail myself." She removed her hand from his arm since they were at the carriage.

He stood before her silently for a moment, just looking at her face. "As do I, Miss Bennet. As do I," he finally said. He glanced to his left and his right. "I do not intend to marry," he said softly.

Horror washed over Mary. He had been thinking she was trying to gain his intention. "I was not..." she stammered. "I do not... I am not a flirt, Mr. Alford."

His eyebrows flew toward his hat. "I did not think you were. I was just clarifying myself so that there could be no misunderstanding."

Mary's troubling emotions tried to push their way forward, demanding that they be released in some way. "Then, we wish the same thing for you," she said curtly. "I had only hoped to be friends with you and your nieces while I am in the area."

"And that is what I wished for as well," he hurried to say.

"Then, it seems we understand each other perfectly, sir." Mary dipped a shallow curtsy. "Thank you, for seeing us to our carriage. Do let me know how the room progresses. I will send the pictures of the chair to Maggie and Rose as soon as I have them complete."

"You are welcome to bring them to Wellworth."

Mary wanted to accept his offer, but her emotions were too high to be perfectly calm. "I think, perhaps, it is best if I do not. We would not wish for anyone to misunderstand our friendship. Good day, Mr. Alford. Give my best to the Miss Alfords."

She turned away from him and walked the few remaining steps to the door of the carriage. Each footfall echoed the same message through her heart. *At least, now you know. At least, now you know.* She did like him as one might like a suitor. She must, for otherwise, his words would not have cut her heart as they had.

Chapter 9

Stuart stood rooted to his spot as the Darcys' carriage began to move away from the church. That had not gone well at all.

"It is good to see you again." An elderly matron who looked familiar to Stuart had approached him. He was nearly certain she had been a friend of his mother, but he was not able to come up with her name.

"Thank you."

"I thought we might never see you again," she continued. "What with how things went before you left us."

"The plan was to not return," he admitted, "but I have responsibilities here now." He cocked his head. "I apologize, Madame, but I am not remembering your name."

His grey-haired companion smiled broadly.

"Would it help you to remember if I mentioned that my cook makes the most delicious chocolate tarts you have ever eaten?"

"Mrs. George! How could I have forgotten your name?"

"How indeed," she said with a laugh. "However, if I had just gotten scolded by a lovely young woman, I might find my mind somewhat befuddled." Her eyebrows flicked upward as if it was a fabulously clever joke that she had just told.

Chocolate tarts and gossip. Yes, those were the hallmarks by which he remembered Mrs. George.

"It is not what you think," he cautioned. He did not need anyone tying him to anyone. He had no plans to marry. Ever. He was not going to willingly place himself in a place where his heart, which he hoped was nearly fully healed, could once again be trampled upon and crushed.

"And what do I think it is?" she asked.

"Miss Bennet is a friend of Maggie and Rose."

"That is not what I thought," she teased.

Stuart shook his head. "No, that is not what you thought, but it is the truth."

"She is not your *friend*?"

He could feel the noose of gossip tightening.

"Miss Bennet is a friend. A new acquaintance, actually. However, she is not a *friend* as you are implying."

"And what am I implying?"

Ah, yes. He remembered now why he linked Mrs. George with chocolate tarts. It was the sole reason he was able to tolerate being in her presence for very long. She was far too good at twisting a story from the mundane into something tantalizingly scandalous with just a few questions and well-placed comments.

He was not, however, a young man trying to please his parents any longer, and so, unlike he might have done before, he decided to answer her directly.

"I believe you know what you were implying, but be that as it may, I will do my utmost to make certain there is no doubt. You were thinking that Miss Bennet and I might be the sort of friends who eventually marry."

Amusement danced behind her spectacles.

"We are not." He made certain to enunciate each word slowly and precisely for emphasis.

"Miss Bennet is a very proper young lady."

"I know she is." A proper young lady he had unwittingly accused of flirting.

Mrs. George fiddled with the edge of her glove and did not meet his eyes when she said, "It would not be a bad thing to pursue a proper young lady this time around."

"I am not pursuing anyone," he replied. "Nor do I have any intentions of pursuing anyone."

That got her eyes to leave her glove and find his.

"Now, I really must be on my way. Maggie and Rose are waiting for me."

She placed a hand on his arm as he attempted to move past her.

"Your nieces have not had a mother for two years, and I am not certain how much of one they had before that. It would be a shame for them to never experience the proper love of a mother."

Mrs. George had never made it a secret that she had not been fond of Sarah, so the disparagement of her falling from Mrs. George's lips was not a surprise. However, it did give Stuart a moment's pause. Had Sarah not been a kind and loving mother? He had always thought she would be, but then, again, he had also thought she loved him and that had not turned out to be true.

"Just consider it," Mrs. George said softly before removing her hand from his arm. "Your mother is not here to say these things to you, and she was such a dear friend. I simply could not live with myself if I thought I had been presented with an opportunity to speak on her behalf and had not taken it."

He was not certain what to say to that. It was not that he did not have a host of thoughts wanting to be shared. It was just that most of them sounded rather ungracious. So rather than sharing any of them, he simply gave her a nod and was on his way.

He had been afraid the gossip mill would be in its delight after Miss Bennet had taken so long to take her seat this morning when entering the church. He had hoped her attention to him would not be noticed, but it, quite obviously, had been. He blew out a breath as he wondered if she were just so naïve that she had not considered gossip to be a danger since she was new to the area, or if she had hoped that there would be someone like Mrs. George in attendance who would link her name with his. Surely, she was not so scheming. Miss Bennet did not strike him as a lady who played games, but he had been played for a fool before.

"Did you ask her?" Maggie said before Stuart could do more than open the door to the carriage.

"No."

"Why?"

"She had to leave before I was able to invite Miss Bennet to visit you." His spirit groaned. There was little hope that Miss Bennet would ever accept an invitation to visit Wellworth Abbey now. He had made certain of that when attempting to drive any thoughts of her interest in him from her head.

Maggie's lower lipped protruded slightly as she looked away from him.

"Miss Bennet has relations with whom she needs to spend time."

Maggie nodded but did not look at him. He had most thoroughly disappointed her.

"She said she will send you the picture of your chair when it is complete."

Maggie looked at him, but he would have rather that she had not. Her eyes were misty, and that protruding lower lip trembled. He swallowed. He wanted to tell her that he would fix things so that her friend would come to visit, but he could not promise what was not possible.

"I am certain we will have other callers," Miss Leslie inserted.

Maggie pressed her lips together and shook her head.

It was a very somber and silent hour in the carriage. One in which Maggie finally sniffled herself to sleep, Rose stared at him with wide distrustful eyes, and he admonished himself most severely for having made a mess of things in such a grand fashion as he had.

~*~*~

Carefully, Stuart lifted the sleeping Maggie from the carriage when they arrived at Wellworth.

She stirred as he settled her against his chest. Her eyes fluttered open. "Papa?" she asked sleepily.

"Uncle Stuart," he whispered.

"I want Papa," she replied.

"I know, sweet pea, but he is not here." He pressed her closer to him. He also longed for Broderick to be with them. With heavy feet, he trudged up the steps into the house and then up more steps as he made his way to the nursery to place his charge in her bed.

"Perhaps you could visit Pemberley," Miss Leslie said to him when she followed him out into the hallway after seeing that both Maggie and Rose were in Mrs. Fenton's care.

"Perhaps," he agreed, though he doubted Miss Bennet would want that.

"Forgive me, sir. I know it is not my place, but did something happen to sever our relationship with Miss Bennet? I only ask so that I can be prepared to face the children."

He grimaced. "I said something that was apparently intolerably stupid, though I truly did not know it would be. I fear Miss Bennet wishes to have nothing further to do with me."

"I see."

"I told her I was not planning to marry," he added in response to Miss Leslie's shocked expression. "She assumed I thought of her as a flirt." He scrubbed his face. "I did not mean to offend her."

"I am certain you did not, sir."

"Thank you, but that does very little to improve me in Maggie's eyes." He shook his head. "She has had so much taken from her, and now I have taken Miss Bennet from her as well. I do not blame her for hating me."

"She does not hate you, sir. She may be greatly displeased at the moment, but it will pass."

"I pray you are correct, Miss Leslie." And he truly did pray the girls' governess was right about that. He had dealt with a lot of unpleasant emotions over the past five years, but the one he currently held in his heart was the worst. He had caused pain to the child who had accepted him so willingly. He had never felt so low. To make matters worse, he knew he had also offended a young lady whom he truly did respect – even if he did not completely trust her motives.

He stopped in the long gallery on his way to his rooms. It was not precisely on his way to his room, but it was not a long detour either. It was just down a short flight of stairs. He stood before his brother's portrait.

"I miss you," he said aloud. "I have for years – even when I hated you, I missed you. I could actually use your help right now." He chuckled bitterly. "I bet you never would have believed that I would ever admit such a thing. I certainly never said it when we were young, but it was always true."

He drew a deep breath and blew it out in a great huff. That was likely why the whole ordeal with Sarah had been so damaging. He and Broderick had always competed with each other, but never to the point of harm like Sarah had caused. The betrayal of a lover paled in comparison to the betrayal of a brother.

"Why?" he asked. "What made you do it? I understand Sarah's reasons were mercenary, but yours?" He shook his head. "I have never understood yours."

He stood for a moment longer in front of his brother before he dried his eyes. "I could really use your help now," he said once more before turning to go to his room.

He had not gone more than five steps, however, before he was struck with a thought. Perhaps Broderick had always needed his help as well. Maybe that was why he had chosen Stuart to care for his daughters. Had it been a natural decision on Broderick's part to just name his brother on whom he had always counted as the protector of his children? Stuart turned and looked back down the length of the long gallery. It was entirely possible. Indeed, he was going to take that as his answer. His brother was relying on him, and so were Maggie and Rose.

He had made a mess of things with Miss Bennet and caused pain to Maggie, but he was not incapable of correcting his errors, was he? He certainly hoped he was not. Miss Leslie was correct. A call at Pemberley seemed to be just the thing that was needed, but it would not be with Maggie and Rose in tow. Tomorrow, he would ride over there and see what could be salvaged of the special relationship his nieces had formed with Miss Bennet. Eventually, they would have to part with her, but it would not be now, nor would it be because of something stupid he had done.

Chapter 10

The sound of a stream gurgling and bubbling around rocks was one of Mary's favourite sounds. Where she sat in this wooded area of Pemberley's park provided her with a wonderful concert of babbling water, accompanied by songbirds.

She closed her eyes and simply breathed as she listened for a few minutes. Perhaps immersing herself in the sounds surrounding her would do what her drawing had not yet been able to do. Today, her heart ached most dreadfully. She would finish her drawings of Maggie's chair tomorrow. She was nearly done with it now, and instead of being excited to deliver the final piece to her young friend, she would not be able to see the look of delight on the child's face when she received it because of her uncle. Her handsome, never-to-be-Mary's, uncle.

Oh, why had she been born looking as she did? Why could she not have been blessed with a tenth of the beauty that Jane had? If she had, then gentlemen would not find it so repulsive to be looked at by her and feel the need to tell her to stop flirting. Not that she had been flirting!

She opened her eyes and applied herself to her current, non-reading-chair sketch once again. She had only been deep in thought yesterday. She had not been staring at Mr. Alford as he seemed to think she had been.

Perhaps she did not need Jane's beauty but rather Lydia's ability to not pay attention to anything for more than a few seconds. Maybe that is what she lacked, for then, she would have seen Maggie's hand safely tucked under her uncle's hand and would have been able to turn away immediately instead of pondering the deeper meaning of such a small gesture.

A branch cracked behind her, and she jumped.

"Miss Bennet?" Mr. Alford sat on his horse looking down the bank at her. "May I water my horse here?"

"It is not my stream, Mr. Alford," she said curtly.

"I did not ask because I thought you owned the

stream. I asked because I did not wish to interrupt your solitude without permission."

Mary drew in a slow breath through her nose. She really should not let her hurt from yesterday keep clouding her behaviour, but it was hard not to do so. "I would not want to refuse your horse refreshment."

He dismounted. "But you would refuse me permission to speak to you?" he asked as he led his horse to the stream.

"We are alone, Mr. Alford. I think it would be best if you just refreshed your animal and left it at that. We would not want someone to come along and devise a story about a secret assignation between us, would we?"

He shook his head. "I am fairly confident no one is going to happen along by chance. I only knew where to find you because your aunt told me where you were."

"My aunt?" Why would her aunt direct a gentleman to her in a secluded spot?

"Yes, your aunt. I was just preparing to leave Pemberley after having spoken to your uncle and Mr. Darcy about my dreadful behaviour towards you yesterday." He stroked the side of his horse and did not look at her. "I did not mean what I said the way it sounded. I would never think of you as a flirt."

Mary chuckled bitterly at that.

"What have I said?" he asked with what sounded like trepidation in his voice.

"No one would ever think of me as a flirt," she replied, giving her thoughts a voice before she could think better of it.

"Why do you say that?"

She rolled her eyes and shook her head. "I thought you were more intelligent than that, Mr. Alford. There are ladies who gentlemen hope to have flirt with them and then there are ladies like me."

His brow furrowed and he took a step away from her. "At the risk of stirring your ire further and being labelled an utter blockhead, I still do not understand."

"It does not matter." She had no desire to explain her plainness to him. "I can assure you that even if I were the sort of lady a gentleman might wish to have flirt with him, I was not flirting with you yesterday before church. I was thinking."

"While staring at me?"

"No. While observing your niece's hand in yours." She lifted her sketchbook to show him what she was drawing. "I wanted to commit it to memory so I could draw it." She shrugged. "I am sorry if I caused you discomfort in the process."

His horse was no longer drinking from the stream, so she smiled at him and said, "I hope your ride back to Wellworth is pleasant."

"It cannot be unless I succeed in my purpose for coming to Pemberley today. That is why your aunt told me where you were. She knows how utterly at a loss I am for fixing things without your help."

It was Mary's turn to be flummoxed by what her companion said. "I am sorry, but I do not understand. How can *I* help *you*?"

He took a seat a few feet away from her. "I will not fault you if you do not wish to forgive me, and though I would rather that you did forgive me, I can bear your displeasure if you will please not allow that anger to separate Maggie from you."

Is that what he thought kept her from visiting Wellworth Abbey – her anger? "It is not my anger that keeps me from seeing your nieces. It is your fear of being thought to court me. I would not wish to be a source of unease for you."

There was some anger. She would not deny that. However, it was more hurt and humiliation that kept her from moving past her angry response from yesterday and conducting life as if the whole incident had never happened.

"I do not fear —"

She held up her hand, cutting off his denial. "Is that not why you informed me that you were never getting married?"

"No," he said in surprise. "I told you I was never marrying because I never am, and I would not want you to assume there was any hope if you did indeed —" He stopped speaking. "You must understand," he said with a wave of his hand. He blew out a breath. "It sounds too arrogant to explain further."

She could not disagree with that, nor would she. Some might try to ease Mr. Alford's embarrassment, which was clearly written on his face as he looked away from her and toward the stream, but Mary was not some. Therefore, though her face burned with the awkwardness of the topic, she would not let it prevent her from being forthright. Misunderstandings were the result of avoiding communication that was thought to be unnecessary or uncomfortable. It felt very much like prevarication to just let a discussion fall away without clarifying her understanding and his.

"You are handsome, and if I were any other lady, I might consider trying to draw you along."

He looked at her warily. "However?"

"I know my shortcomings, sir, and I attempt to dwell within reality."

From the look on his face, she was not helping to clear anything up. In fact, it appeared she was making things less clear.

"I am not the sort of lady you or any other gentleman like yourself would consider for his wife." There, she had said it.

"Why?"

Had he just asked why? Truly, she had not thought he lacked intelligence, but perhaps that was why he was not married nor wished to ever marry.

"Do you wear spectacles to read?" she asked. It seemed more polite to question his eyesight before questioning his mind.

He shook his head. "No. I see quite well."

Well, that removed that excuse from him, but if it was not his eyesight, then, perhaps it was his ability to notice things. "Have you looked at me?"

"I am looking at you now."

"What colour are my eyes?"

"Blue with some gold flecks," he answered without taking a moment to study her eyes, which meant he had noticed details about her before now.

That left only one option. There must be something lacking in his mind. It was a pity. Hopefully, he would still be able to raise his nieces as they needed to be raised.

"You have not answered my question. I see no reason why you would not be the sort of lady a gentleman such as myself would look for as a wife – if I were the sort looking for a wife, which I am not."

"Most gentlemen prefer pretty, lively ladies who paint screens and discuss fashion and can play the piano and do not question what they are told."

What could only be described as disbelief washed over his face. "You think that I am the sort of man who values a wife as only a beautiful accessory?"

"No," Mary answered frankly. "You do not wish for a wife. You have made that abundantly clear. Therefore, I do not think of you as one of those sorts of gentlemen. However, when it comes to other gentlemen like yourself who are agreeable to marriage? Yes, I think that."

"That seems harsh."

Mary shrugged. "Life and truth are not always gentle."

His brow furrowed and he shook his head before beginning to laugh.

"I do not see what is so humorous, Mr. Alford," Mary said when his laughter grew louder rather than subsiding.

"You," he managed to say between peals of laughter.

"If you came to seek my forgiveness, you are doing an exceptionally poor job of it."

He slowly stopped laughing. "You, Miss Bennet, are a delightful oddity."

"You are still not succeeding." The use of the word delightful before the word oddity did not make the word flattering.

"I hope my nieces grow up to be ladies who think as clearly as you do, Miss Bennet."

Mary opened her mouth to reply but closed it again, as she was not sure what to say. He considered her a good example of what a lady should be? There might indeed be something wrong with his faculties, but she wasn't certain if it was a good something or a bad something.

"Am I still failing?" he asked in a teasing tone.

"Not utterly," she replied, causing him to chuckle.

"Will you please call at Wellworth Abbey? My nieces would be overjoyed if you did, and I would be happy for it."

Oh, she wanted to. She dearly wanted to. But... "There will be those who will whisper," she cautioned.

"I know. Your uncle and Mr. Darcy have already stressed that to me, and I will tell you what I told them. While I am not fond of the idea of having my name linked with anyone's." He held her gaze and repeated the word *anyone's* before continuing. "I can bear it for the sake of my nieces. They have had so much taken from them, that I cannot let my wishes to not be gossiped about take anything else from them, especially when it is their dear friend."

Mary pressed her lips together to keep them from trembling and blinked against the tears his pleading wished to pull from her for it made her feel valued, if only for a moment.

"Please, please, say you will bring your drawings to the girls and not send them by messenger."

"I will eventually leave Derbyshire."

He nodded. "I realize that, but when you are separated from them at that time, it will be because of how life goes. And there might be the hope of your writing to them?" he asked hopefully. "I cannot fail them in this, Miss Bennet. My brother left them to my care, and I will not fail him or them. If you cannot call at Wellworth, I will bring them to you at Pemberley."

He was handsome. Mary had always been aware of that, but as he sat before her begging her to make his nieces happy, he became even more attractive. Granting him his wish would certainly cause her an enormous amount of pain when she eventually had to walk away from both him and his nieces.

"Please, Miss Bennet."

"I have missed them," she admitted.

He smiled. "And Maggie was heartbroken and more than a little displeased with me when I could not assure her that you would visit her."

She looked up at the canopy of leaves above her. Life was not always gentle, but she knew what needed to be done. She must brave the pain that lay in her future to provide what the Miss Alfords and their uncle needed now. She nodded. "I will have their drawings ready on the day after tomorrow."

"I can bring the girls to you," he offered quickly when she paused. "They might like to play in the stream."

"Very well, Mr. Alford. I will allow you to bring your nieces for a visit." She gasped. "I should likely ask Mr. Darcy first."

Mr. Alford chuckled and shook his head. "He was agreeable to either your going to Wellworth or our coming to Pemberley."

"You discussed that?"

"Yes."

"Then, tell Maggie and Rose that I eagerly await their visit."

He stood and held out a hand to help her to her feet. "Nothing would make me happier. Are you returning to the house now?"

"I am."

"May we," he motioned to his horse, "escort you part way? I am curious about the drawing on which you are currently working."

"If we are seen walking together, there may be whispers," she cautioned.

He extended his arm to her. "I think I can survive the storm to assuage my curiosity and to have something to share with Maggie when I get home."

"In that case," she placed her hand on his arm, "I would enjoy the company." Far more than she likely should, but there was no help for it. Sacrifices had to be made in the course of helping others, did they not?

Chapter 11

Maggie skipped ahead of Stuart with Rose's hand firmly grasped in hers. Both girls had decided once again that they liked him, though Rose still harbored trepidation in her eyes when she looked at him as if she could not get past the idea that he had been the source of her sister's tears on Sunday. No amount of reassurances from himself or Miss Leslie seemed enough to calm her fears that he would once again cause her sister pain.

The girls stopped at the foot of the stairs that led up to Pemberley's door and waited for him to join them. Then, they followed him up the steps.

"Are you ready?" he whispered, crouching down, and looking each of his nieces in the eye.

They both nodded eagerly. Maggie was currently silent, but ever since he had returned home two days ago and told her about the upcoming visit to

Pemberley, she had been an absolute chatterbox about her friend Miss Bennet and what she hoped would happen today.

"Best behaviour?" he asked as a reminder of Miss Leslie's instructions before they had climbed into the carriage at Wellsworth. Miss Leslie was to have the day to herself. Harriet and Susan, the two nursery maids, had been sent as companions for the girls should their services be required.

Again, both heads bobbed up and down.

"You will say *good day* and *thank you* and other such things?" he asked Rose with a wink.

Her little mouth turned up into a smile that shone in her eyes. "Yes," she replied.

"I am very happy to hear it." Stuart stood and smoothed his jacket. He was not entirely certain why he felt as nervous as he did. But there were butterflies having quite the raucous party in his stomach. He silently told them to leave off as he lifted the brass knocker and let it fall with a thud.

Something pulled at the edge of his coat's tails, and looking down, he saw Rose standing at his side with her hand firmly grasping the material of his coat. Maggie still stood beside her sister, holding her hand. Could it be that he was not so far from being trusted by Rose as he thought he was? That thought seemed to do a better job of quieting his nerves than the scold he had given them had.

The door in front of them opened, and soon they were all gathered inside, following Pemberley's butler to the drawing room.

"Do you want to hold my hand?" Stuart offered Rose.

She shook her head and kept her grip on his jacket. Apparently, holding his hand was a step too far in trusting him and one that she was not yet willing to give him.

"Mr. Alford, Miss Margaret Alford, and Miss Rose Alford," the butler announced.

When Stuart stepped into the room, his coattail followed, but not immediately, because Rose was somewhat reticent to greet everyone gathered. That is, she was reticent until she saw Miss Bennet. Then, Stuart found his coat freed so that Rose could do her duty in waving to her friend.

"We are delighted to have you visit us today." Mrs. Darcy crossed the room to greet Stuart and his nieces. Her husband remained where he was with his relations and sister. "Was it a long drive?" she asked his nieces.

"Yes," Rose answered, peeking up at Stuart for approval, which he gave in the form of a nod.

"We will have some lemonade and biscuits in the garden later, but first, I think my sister Mary has something special to show you." She held out one hand to each girl and was rewarded with a small hand placed inside her proffered one. "Mary thought it would be best if your uncle sat with my husband and uncle while she showed you your pictures. That way, you can have the honour of showing the drawing to your uncle later as a surprise."

"Did she, indeed?" Stuart asked

"She did."

"That was very thoughtful."

Mrs. Darcy smiled. "You will find there are few who are more thoughtful than my sister. I do not believe that even Jane puts as much thought into things as Mary does."

"I have noticed she thinks more deeply," and differently, "than most."

"She is special." There appeared to be a hopeful glint in Mrs. Darcy's eye.

"I will not refute that, and I am certain that some fellow will be fortunate to secure her someday." Stuart emphasized the words *some fellow* and hoped that Mrs. Darcy would hear the gentle reminder that he was not in the market for a wife.

Her head tipped to one side as she looked at him. "I do hope he will. It would be a pity if he did not recognize her for her worth."

"Indeed, it would."

"As long as we are agreed."

He was not certain they did agree, for that hopeful glint in Mrs. Darcy's eye had not faded. He had been warned by Mr. Darcy and Mr. Gardiner that while their wives would be told that he was only calling on Miss Bennet for the sake of his nieces, there would be no stopping the ladies from hoping for more. Apparently, the gentlemen had not spoken based on anything other than the truth.

"Shall we go see Mary?" she asked Maggie and Rose.

"Yes, please," the two chorused.

He watched as they were willingly led to the far side of the generous drawing room where he could see drawings lying on a table in front of a sofa.

"Miss Bennet," he called to Mary as she and Miss Darcy moved to join her sister and his nieces.

She stopped and looked at him.

"Thank you."

She gave him a simple nod and then continued on her way.

"Your nieces are fortunate to have you," Mrs. Gardiner said as Stuart joined her, her husband, and Mr. Darcy.

"They seem to think so today, but until I returned home on Monday, they would have disagreed most heartily with your statement."

Mr. Gardiner chuckled. "The loyalty of a child can be easily swayed at times."

Stuart cast a look across the room at his nieces. "Not all of them," he said. "Rose is still reluctant to accept me completely."

"There are those who are more timid," Mrs. Gardiner agreed. "Of our five nieces, Mary and Kitty always hung back the most when they were young. Kitty was fortunate to have a sister who pulled her forward."

"Mary was left to find her own way," Mr. Gardiner added.

"And my poor, unfortunate sister only had me, and I am not one to enter into conversation or company with any sort of eagerness or great finesse," Mr. Darcy said with a laugh. "However, Georgiana has learned to outshine me and has helped draw me forward – as did my friend Bingley and my cousin Richard. And now, I have my wife to ease me into situations."

"Have you ever been stricken with a similar malady to Mr. Darcy, or have you always been of the charmed and charming sort, Mr. Alford?" Mrs. Gardiner asked.

"While I would not call myself either charmed or charming, I have never found it difficult to enter new situations until recently. I nearly always had a brother or friend at my side. Even now, I have a brother who is willing to help me find my way in my new role, and Broderick left me Miss Leslie, who I must say is a treasure. I am certain I would be making a much greater muddle of things if I did not have her there to correct the things I say to Maggie and Rose."

Even when he attempted to choose his words carefully, he still found himself saying things in the wrong way. He was beginning to think that speaking to young misses like his nieces was more difficult than composing a paper in Latin or Greek for a professor. Theirs was a truly foreign language to him which was made more difficult because it sounded the same as the language he spoke.

"Well, I, for one, think you are succeeding." Mrs. Gardiner gave him a kind smile. It was the sort of smile a mother might bestow on a child who had done a job well. "Not every gentleman would risk his reputation as a confirmed bachelor for the sake of his charges."

"Madeline, you promised," Mr. Gardiner said quietly.

"I have not said a word about anything," she assured him.

On that Stuart would say she was correct. She had not said he might be less confirmed in his bachelorhood than he thought he was, but he could hear it lying just beneath her words.

"Mary mentioned that you thought your nieces would enjoy playing in the stream near where you found her yesterday," Mrs. Gardiner said.

"I did mention that to Miss Bennet because I remember venturing into the cool water of a stream on a warm summer's day and quite enjoying it as a child."

"I cannot fathom a child who would not like something like that, but I suppose there are a few who would not," Mrs. Gardiner agreed. "I could see a child not liking the feel of the squishy things that grow in the stream or the slippery feel of the rocks."

"I suppose you are correct." He had not even considered that a child might not enjoy getting wet. He and his brothers had always delighted in a splash in a pond or stream.

"I had a couple of my old boats brought down from the storerooms," Mr. Darcy inserted. "Even a child who does not want to get her feet wet might enjoy sailing a boat."

The thoughtfulness and welcoming nature of such a gesture was not lost on Stuart. It was as if he and his nieces had been taken into this family.

"Thank you. I am not even sure what toys from my childhood still remain at Wellworth. I have not looked." He would have to make a point of checking into that. There were a few things that he would not be opposed to seeing placed in the nursery for the girls to use if they had not been already.

"I am happy to be of service. Everything we thought you might need has been placed in a donkey cart that is big enough for two tired young girls to ride in if it becomes necessary."

"That is an excellent idea." Stuart had not even considered what he would do if both Maggie and

Rose became tired before they returned home. He could carry one, but he doubted he could carry both.

"I wish I could say it was mine, but it was not," Mr. Darcy said.

Stuart looked at Mrs. Gardiner, who shook her head.

"That was Mary's idea," she replied.

Again, Stuart heard what was not said. Miss Bennet would make a wonderful mother for his nieces.

"Is something wrong?" Mr. Gardiner asked.

Stuart shook his head. Nothing was wrong other than he had just considered Miss Bennet as his wife and had not been abhorred by the thought of having one.

"Are you certain?"

His face must have registered his shock in realizing that the thought of taking a wife did not cause his stomach to twist and his pulse to race. It was a realization that was just as unexpected as his not having felt anger for Sarah when seeing her portrait had been.

"Nothing is amiss." He lied. "I am just wondering if I have remembered everything I need, but I am sure between Mrs. Fenton and Miss Leslie, as well as Harriet and Susan, there is nothing which has been forgotten that might be required."

"If there is, I am certain my housekeeper can find something to suffice," Mr. Darcy assured him.

"Uncle Stuart," Maggie stood just to his right with Mrs. Darcy behind her. "May we, please, go to the garden?"

"Yes, of course." He stood and so did the others in his group. "Did you like your pictures?"

She nodded vigorously as a smile spread across her face. "We decided not to show you until we get to the carriage." She pressed her fingers to her lips as if attempting to keep from giggling.

"I have to wait until the end of the day?"

She nodded and this time she did giggle.

"They both thought it would be a fabulous joke to play on you." Mrs. Darcy looked just as amused as his niece. He suspected there was a great deal of playfulness contained within her.

"And it is," he agreed as Maggie took his hand and Mrs. Darcy took her husband's arm.

Darcy pulled his wife closer to his side than most would likely consider proper, but it did not bother Stuart. His father and mother had been the same way. That is not to say he was not surprised by the action, for he had not thought that Darcy would be so, nor had Stuart thought Mr. Darcy would marry someone so lively as Mrs. Darcy appeared to be. Indeed, Stuart had always expected the gentleman to have a quiet and reserved wife and settle into a companionable and completely proper relationship. Yet, here was Darcy being what some might deem improper and appearing to be more than just companions with his wife. It was as if his love for her had reached through his well-known reserve and pulled him forward.

Stuart's lips curled up on their own at the thought. It was as Aaron had said. One part of the pair before him complemented the other and likely brought out the other's best.

This thought about his brother quite naturally turned his thoughts to the question Aaron had posed about Stuart's relationship with Sarah. How would this scene have played out if Sarah were here with him? He had to consider it if he ever wanted to return to his brother and share his finding so that he could then press Aaron to tell him what he had meant by playing brother against brother.

Behind him, Miss Bennet and Miss Darcy walked with Rose, and the Gardiners followed behind them.

Sarah would not be behind Stuart talking to a child. He had never once seen her engage with any of the children who had been at various events. For a moment, he wondered once again about Mrs. George's comments about Maggie and Rose not truly having had a mother. Had Sarah ignored them? The thought made his heart ache for them, but he knew the truth of the matter in an instant as he imagined where Sarah would be in this gathering.

Unless she had changed considerably since the last time they had been in town for the season, which was just two months before she had announced her betrothal to his brother, she would in this current tableau be as near as she could be to Mr. Darcy because he was the gentleman with the most income in the room. It had never mattered to her if a wealthy gentleman was married or not, she had flirted with anyone who was not known to have squandered their fortune.

Stuart had jealously teased her about it at one point, asking her if she were applying to be the fellow's mistress, and she had assured him that she would never be anyone's mistress. However, she had taunted, wives sometimes did not outlive their husbands. Then, when he had voiced his shock at her reply, she had placated him with the assurance that she was only making certain that he had the best connections and was offered the best position he could find. And, like a fool, he had believed her.

Oh, how stupid he had been! He could now see, as clear as clear could be, that he had been no more than a pawn in her game of flirtations – someone to keep her company and make her feel adored as she sought a more advantageous match. How blind he had been! How utterly blind! He vowed to himself, as he stepped through Pemberley's garden doors, that he would never be so again. Tomorrow, he would take his newfound wisdom to his brother and hopefully discover what secrets Aaron held.

Chapter 12

A miniature boat bobbed along on the currents of the stream while a sweet young girl guided it along with the string that was attached to its bow.

"You are very good at keeping it away from the rocks," Mary said to Rose as the two of them found a place on the bank of the stream from which to sail Rose's boat.

Maggie had been eager to divest herself of her socks and shoes and take a walk in the shallow part of the stream. Rose had looked terrified at the idea of walking in the water. Not even Maggie's pleas were enough to shake Rose from her position of keeping her feet securely in her shoes and on dry land.

A short distance away from where Mary sat with Rose, Maggie and her uncle were picking their way cautiously along the edge of the stream.

"Oh, look!" Mr. Alford cried, pointing toward the middle of the stream. "He would make a tasty meal. Did you see the fish?"

"No," Maggie replied.

"He is right over there." Again, her uncle pointed toward the deeper part of the stream.

"She may be too short to see it," Mary offered when Maggie still insisted that she could not see the fish.

"Good thought. Here, Maggie, let me lift you."

"But you will get wet!" Maggie protested.

"A little, but not overly." He bent towards her. "Wrap your arms around my neck," he instructed as he lifted her. "Put your cheek against mine and look where I am looking."

"Oh! I see it! I see it!" Maggie peeked over her uncle's shoulder. "There is a fish right there, Rose!" She cried. "You should see it."

Rose shook her head furiously.

"It looks just like the ones Cook has in the kitchen sometimes, Rose, but those do not wiggle like this one is doing."

Rose continued to shake her head. There was nothing that was going to coax her into the water.

"Maybe it will swim over here," Mary said.

"Or maybe Mr. Darcy will catch it," Mr. Alford said.

Uncle Gardiner and Mr. Darcy had walked out with Mary and the Alfords when they had left the garden but had stopped a distance away to try to catch any of the fish that might get scared in their direction by the splashing and playing of the children. Mary could just see them through the trees.

She had been happy for their willingness to act as chaperones so that no one would be able to say anything about Mr. Alford being alone with her. She would hate for rumours to begin that would force Mr. Alford to offer for her to protect her reputation.

Mr. Alford had been certain that they would not need a chaperone beyond the girls' nursemaids, and he was likely correct. However, Mary had wished to make certain that nothing could be said, and with that in mind, she had asked her uncle last night if he wanted to go fishing.

Mr. Darcy had thought it was an excellent suggestion, and he had added that it might be fun if they all went along to the stream. Not everyone had thought that was a good idea. Aunt Gardiner and Elizabeth had thought it best if they did not overwhelm the children, and so, it was just Uncle Gardiner and Mr. Darcy who had accompanied them today.

"Do you like to eat fish?" Mary asked Rose.

The youngster looked away from her boat and toward Mary. "Yes." The smile she wore spoke to how much the child liked to eat fish.

"I do, too. In fact, it is one of my favourite things to eat. Do you have a favourite thing to eat?"

The question was met with a stretch of silence before Rose made her reply of cake.

Mary chuckled. "Cake is delicious."

She used the long stick she held to draw Rose's boat up the stream so that it could once again sail down to where she and Rose were sitting.

Glancing toward Mr. Alford, she saw that Maggie had been returned to the water and was holding her skirt high so she could bend down to look at something with her uncle. Mary knew she should look away quickly – it had been being captivated by how that gentleman interacted with his niece which had caused her current heartache, after all – but the sight of Mr. Alford crouching down and fishing something out of the water was too enjoyable for her to do as she ought. She sighed. Every time he did something sweet for his nieces, she found that he grew more and more attractive to her.

"A newt." He held out his hand to show what he had captured to her and Rose. Then, he moved in their direction. "See, Rose. This is a newt." The creature passed from one of his hands to the other as he kept moving his hands to give the newt somewhere to scurry. "Do you see it?"

Rose nodded.

"Do you think you are brave enough to touch it?"

Rose did not look as if she was.

"I am," Mary offered. Perhaps if Rose saw her touch it, it would help her be less timid.

Mr. Alford splashed his way over to Mary.

"Miss Bennet," he said as he presented the creature to her. "Do you want to hold it?"

Mary put out her hand. She truly had no desire to hold a newt, but one sometimes did what one did not want to do when one wished to encourage bravery in another.

"Oh, it tickles," she said with a nervous laugh when the newt scampered across her hand and back into Mr. Alford's, which he had moved so that the creature would not be lost. Then, he lowered his hand to the water and let the newt slip away.

"He is gone back to find more food," he said to Rose as he washed his hands off in the stream. "Are you enjoying your boat?"

"It floats fast."

"I can see that." He waded out a little deeper and pulled the boat up the stream. "I should get back to Maggie, but maybe we can sail boats with you?"

There was still one boat in the cart. Mr. Darcy had made certain that there would be enough for each child and at least one adult to have a ship to command. The delight in Mr. Darcy's eyes when he brought out his old toys and began to tell stories about him and his cousins playing in this very stream had been startling to Mary, but she had been learning, as the weeks passed while she was at Pemberley, that the Mr. Darcy whom everyone saw in public was not the same as the Mr. Darcy who was at ease in his home. She could more easily understand how Elizabeth could love him as much as she did, and she knew she was part of the special few who got to witness him in such a fashion. Of course, his marrying Elizabeth had likely played a substantial role in his more relaxed nature. No one could be ill-at-ease for long when with Elizabeth.

Mary wished she possessed the skill Elizabeth did for making people feel comfortable, but she was Mary and somewhat awkward in company.

Rose scooted closer to her.

The action caused Mary to smile and amend her contemplations. She was awkward in company with adults. As she had discovered on this trip, she was not at all awkward around children. In fact, she found that spending time with Maggie and Rose was perhaps the most enjoyable thing she had ever done. Neither of them judged Mary for being direct or questioning things or just sitting quietly. Children – at least, these two children – were very accepting of differences. Even Rose, with her tendency to be shy, had welcomed Mary with alacrity.

"We have come to join you," Mr. Alford, still without socks or boots on, claimed a place on the stream's bank next to Mary while Maggie joined her sister. "Here you go, Maggie. Try not to let the boats' lines get tangled." He reached across Mary and passed the string he held under Rose's string to Maggie.

"Are you enjoying yourself, Miss Bennet?" He

placed the boat he held on the bank next to him instead of in the water.

"I feel as delighted as the birds sound," she replied.

"Then, we are of one mind on that." He leaned back on his hands while his toes flicked up and down in the water. "I have not enjoyed a good romp in a stream for years." He turned his head towards her. "Sadly, one grows out of such frivolity."

"I am afraid I must disagree with you."

"You must?" he said in surprise.

"Yes, I must."

"Why?"

"Because it is my belief that we do not grow beyond the capability to enjoy life as a child does, but it is rather that we decide to put those enjoyments to the side for a time when other responsibilities claim our attention."

His lips curled into a smile. "Perhaps you are correct."

"Perhaps?" She pressed her lips together. She had not meant to say that aloud.

He laughed. "Very well. You *are* correct. There is no *perhaps* about it."

"You are fortunate, you know," she said.

"How so?"

"You have been given a reason to pick up the enjoyments of youth once again. Not that the way in which you were given the reason was fortunate," she added quickly when she realized how her words could be taken.

"I would not think that you meant what you assume I might think you meant."

Her brow furrowed. "Thank you?"

He chuckled. "I was commending you. You are too kind to have thought the death of a brother was a fortunate thing – no matter what blessings have now been deposited in my care." He drew and released a breath. "Broderick would have loved to be here today. He liked playing in the water even more than Aaron and I did." He sat forward and looked around Mary. "Maggie, did your father ever take you to play in the pond at Wellworth?"

She shook her head. "Mama did not like it."

"Did she not?" Mr. Alford sounded entirely shocked by that.

"She said that once." Her face scrunched up. "Or I think she did. I was little."

Mary pressed her lips together to keep from

smiling. Maggie was still little. She might not be as young as she once was, but she was still little.

"And he never took you by himself after your mother died?"

Maggie shook her head.

"He loved playing in the water when he was a boy," Mr. Alford said. "He and I and Uncle Aaron used to go swimming in the pond at Wellworth. I could teach you how to swim if you want."

"You could?"

There was no little amount of excitement in Maggie's voice.

"I could," her uncle assured her. "I think your Papa would like to know you learned how to swim." He looked at Rose. "I could also teach you."

Rose shook her head and scooted closer to Mary.

"Do you swim, Miss Bennet?"

Apparently, he was going to attempt to use her to persuade his niece to take him up on his offer.

"I do not."

His eyes grew wide. "Is it something girls do not learn to do?" he whispered.

"No, it is something I did not learn to do. Elizabeth and Lydia are both excellent swimmers. Jane is passable, but Kitty and I would likely drown if our boat capsized in deep water."

"Then, I have not offered something I should not have offered?"

He was looking at her with such concern that she could not help but smile at his expression. "No, you have not offered to allow them to do anything improper."

"Thank you. I would offer to teach you to swim, but I *know* that would be improper."

Mary laughed nervously. "Indeed, it would be. It would also be impossible. My lack of ability is not due to a lack of instruction." She shrugged when he looked at her in surprise. "It is just not a skill of which I am capable."

His feet flicked in and out of the water. "I have not gone swimming in years." His eyes were once again looking toward the sky. "Broderick and I would sneak out to go swimming every year before we left for the autumn term of school."

"He sounds like he was a good brother."

Mr. Alford sighed heavily. "He was at one time."

"But not always?"

He smiled uneasily at her. "My nose is not straight."

"Oh! I had forgotten about that." How foolish of her not to remember that story. It had made her quite ill to hear it as she imagined the pain of being kicked by a horse. "Is that the only reason he was not a good brother?"

He shook his head. "No, but I am trying to forget the rest for the sake of his girls."

It was a curious answer, and though she wished to press for more information, she did not. If he wanted to forget something that had happened between him and his brother, she was not going to try to pull those painful memories to the fore just to satisfy her curiosity.

"Elizabeth always says to remember the past only as it gives us pleasure." She leaned forward and used her stick to draw first, Rose's boat upstream and then, Maggie's while the girls tossed bits of twigs and leaves in the water to watch them float away. This was a day she would remember with pleasure once it could be recalled in the future without a pang of regret.

"I think that is an excellent philosophy."

She turned her head so she could study his handsome features and add them to her memories.

Would she ever be able to remember him without regret?

"Maybe it is and maybe it is not," she said. "Or perhaps it is best in some situations, such as yours, and not in others where the events of the past must not be forgotten, or the pleasure of the present may disappear."

His brow furrowed as he shook his head slightly. "How can remembering something unpleasant bring pleasure?"

She lifted a shoulder and let it fall. "I am not entirely certain, but do you feel your good health more fully when you are always well or after you have been ill? Would not the remembrance of your illness make your enjoyment of your health that much more acute?"

One eyebrow arched. "How do you think of these things?"

"How do you not?" She pressed her lips together. "Forgive me," she muttered. What was it about him that made thoughts pop out of her mouth so easily?

His hand touched her elbow when she looked away. "I am not offended," he said when she looked back at him, "and I do not mean to offend you. However, your way of thinking is..." he paused.

"Odd?" It seemed to be the word he often used when describing her.

He shook his head. "Rare." His lips curled up on one side into a sly smile. "One might even say priceless." His tone was teasing.

She wished it were true. She would give anything to have someone like him think of her as priceless. She blinked at the tears that sprang to her eyes.

He sat forward. Concern suffused his features. "What did I say?" he asked. "Please, do not cry. Rose will never forgive me," he added quickly.

"I am merely being maudlin."

"About what?"

"It is nothing for you to be concerned about," she said with a shake of her head. "I get this way when thinking sometimes. It is just another one of my oddities." She attempted to laugh, but it did not sound light and easy as she had hoped it would. Instead, it was a rather pitiful sound.

"It might be fun to walk the boats down the stream a ways, do you not think?" She began to move to get up.

He grasped her arm. "Not until I am certain I have not injured you."

"You have not injured me. I am well."

"Truly?" His expression was one of disbelief.

"Yes." She forced herself to hold his gaze and smile.

His eyes searched hers for a moment as he leaned towards her. His gaze flicked to her lips when she pressed them together. Then, he shook his head and released her arm.

"Allow me to get my boots and Maggie's shoes before we begin our excursion." He looked away as he said it.

"Of course. You can get Maggie's shoes and stockings, and I will help her put them on."

He looked back at her with a perplexed expression before rising from his place and going to retrieve his and Maggie's things.

Chapter 13

Aaron looked up from his reading as Stuart entered his study. "Is it Friday already?" he asked as he placed a marker in his book and closed it.

"No, it is Thursday." Stuart dropped into the chair next to his younger brother. "This could not wait, nor could it be discussed while Rose and Maggie played nearby."

He was not even sure he was truly prepared to discuss it without children in the room. However, if he wanted to get some amount of peace, he needed to talk to Aaron and discover whatever secrets he held regarding the last woman Stuart had thought he had loved. Surely, he was not mistaken this time. Not as he was last time.

Aaron laid his book on the table that stood between these two chairs. "Do you wish for some refreshment? Perhaps a glass of port?"

"At this time in the morning?" Stuart asked in surprise. He had only ever seen Aaron have a glass of port after dinner.

Aaron chuckled. "Yes. It is not the first time I have enjoyed a glass while pondering things I have read." He had risen and was looking down at Stuart. "Your expression makes me think we are going to be speaking about things which might pair well with port rather than some other beverage. Do you want a glass?"

That made sense. Some topics of conversation did seem to pair well with something more full-bodied than tea, and Stuart's thoughts about Miss Bennet had his nerves on edge – so on edge that he had not slept well last night. For those reasons, he nodded his acceptance.

Aaron moved to a cabinet that stood behind his desk. "What urgent matters bring you to see me today?" He bent to retrieve a bottle of port and two glasses.

"She is not Sarah," Stuart blurted. He was certain that there was a more elegant way to broach the subject, but since his mind had not shown him the courtesy of a gentle dawning but had, instead, slapped him with the very words he had just uttered, he thought it was perhaps best to start this discussion in a similar fashion.

Aaron stood slowly and turned toward Stuart with a bottle of port in one hand and two wine glasses hanging between the fingers of his other hand. A small and very satisfied smile crept across his face. "Who is not Sarah?"

Stuart rolled his eyes. "As if you do not know."

Aaron's lips curled into a much broader grin. "I would hate to make a faulty assumption." He removed the stopper from the bottle of port and poured some into the glasses he had placed on his desk. "So, humour me, and answer my question."

"Miss Bennet. She is not Sarah."

"Yes, I know." He picked up the glasses of port and brought Stuart's to him. "What has brought on this obvious realization?"

Instead of retaking his seat as Stuart expected him to do, Aaron placed his glass of port on top of his closed book and went back to his desk.

"I nearly kissed her."

Aaron stopped rummaging through the drawer he had opened and gave Stuart his full attention. Apparently, that was not a reply he had been expecting.

"I have not wanted to kiss anyone as much as I wanted to kiss her," Stuart continued.

"Not even Sarah?"

Stuart shook his head. "Not in the same way. I cannot explain it further than that. I have tried to put it into words, but I have not been successful." He cradled his glass in his hands, staring into it and remembering how drawn to Miss Bennet he had felt yesterday on the bank of that stream. It had been similar to the pull he had felt the other day in that drawing room between the library and music room, only stronger. It had startled him in the drawing room, but it had frightened him yesterday because, yesterday, the glimpse of a happy future which he had seen in the drawing room had also appeared, but it had been so vivid, so clear.

And then... And then, the sight of her teary eyes had cut to his soul as easily as Maggie's had on Sunday, and it was not because he feared Rose would never forgive him. It was because he feared losing Miss Bennet more than anything.

"I have only known her for a few weeks," he muttered more to himself than his brother. "It is not logical to..." He blew out a breath as that word, which had circled his mind all evening and night, reappeared.

"It is not logical to what?" Aaron took his seat again.

"What is that?" Stuart asked when he noticed the book his brother held.

"A journal. Now, answer my question."

There was a B and an A engraved on the front of the journal.

"Is that Broderick's?"

Aaron sighed. "Yes, but I am not sharing anything from it with you until you have finished with your musings. Tell me what is not logical." He tucked the book behind his back and picked up his glass of port.

"I could take it from you." It would not be the first time he had wrestled something away from one of his brothers.

"I know, but if you do, I will tell Maggie."

Stuart laughed. "And what will you tell her?"

"That you hurt me."

"I would not hurt you."

"You might. It would not be the first time you have. I remember many bumps and bruises from wrestling when we were growing up. You gave me fewer than Broderick did, but I did not always come out unscathed from our battles."

"Neither did I," Stuart said with a grin.

"What is not logical?" Aaron repeated.

Stuart's grin did not fade as he shook his head at his brother's unwavering focus. He drew a breath and released it slowly. Only then, did he allow his smile to falter as the unsettling thoughts of yesterday afternoon, evening, and night returned to the fore.

"It is not logical for me to love Miss Bennet." He took a large swallow of his port. "Or anyone for that matter. As I said, we have only known one another for a short time, and I was not even entertaining the idea of loving anyone ever again. But there that word was when I got home from Pemberley yesterday, emblazoned on my mind in large letters and attached to an image of Miss Bennet." He looked at Aaron. "Have I taken leave of my senses?"

Aaron laughed. "No, I would say that you finally found them."

He pulled the journal from behind his back. "Before I show you what is in here, I need to know what it was which made you conclude that Miss

Bennet is not Sarah – and by that, I assume you to mean she is not like Sarah in character. Do I assume correctly?"

"You do." Stuart took another draught from his glass before cradling it in his hands again and staring into the dark liquid it contained. "I was first struck yesterday by how well Darcy and his wife get on. They seem to be two parts of a whole. One does not outshine the other. Indeed, one defers to the other with ease."

"Theirs is a happy marriage," Aaron agreed.

"The Gardiners seem to be the same."

"From what I have seen of them, I would agree."

It was good to hear that his observations were correct and that his opinions had not been formed in error.

"How does that pertain to Miss Bennet not being Sarah?" Aaron asked when Stuart did not continue with his thoughts right away.

"As the call progressed and we were going to the garden, I imagined how Sarah would have been in our gathering." He smiled sheepishly at his brother. "I was trying to do what you suggested. I was comparing Sarah to the happy couples I had been conversing with."

"I am happy to hear my advice was being followed."

"It often is," Stuart replied.

Aaron raised a skeptical brow at the comment.

"I said often not always," Stuart said. "While I was taking your advice, I made note of how Miss Bennet was happy to entertain our nieces. I know Sarah would have been slyly flirting with Darcy." He shook his head at his stupidity. "She used to flirt with all the gentlemen of rank and fortune in town. She claimed it was to help me find the best position for my career, but I doubt that was true."

Aaron made a displeased huffing sound that lent his agreement to what Stuart was saying.

"She was searching for the most advantageous match for herself. I was just her escort to the functions where she could do her hunting."

Aaron shook his head. "You were more than that. You were part of her plan, but continue."

How was he supposed to continue with his thoughts when they had been captured by Aaron's curious statement?

"I assume Miss Bennet was not flirting with her brother-in-law," Aaron prompted when Stuart took too long to considering what Aaron's comment meant.

Stuart's eyes narrowed. "Miss Bennet does not flirt – and to even hint at her flirting with her sister's husband is disturbing."

"It most certainly is," Aaron replied with a grin. "What happened next?"

The annoying fellow certainly knew how to capture Stuart's attention and turn it back to where he wanted it to be.

"We had tea in the garden where Miss Bennet – very patiently – answered all of Maggie's questions and listened to her thoughts as if they were the most important things in the world." He smiled as he remembered the scene. "And Rose would not leave her side. Rose. Who shies away from everyone, including me – though not as much as she once did." It still surprised him just how comfortable Rose appeared to be with Miss Bennet.

"Whenever we were at a gathering that included them – not that we were at many where children were present," he continued. "Sarah did not interact with the children."

"No, she was not fond of children," Aaron agreed.

"Not even her own?"

"Sadly, no. They, like everyone else, were a means to an end."

Stuart's heart broke a bit at having his fears confirmed. "Was she unkind to the girls?"

Aaron shook his head. "She played her part perfectly when they were present. It was only when they were not with her that her true nature was on display – and then, only for those like Broderick who were close to her. I likely should not say it, but Broderick was not utterly devastated when she died. He was not complacent, mind you, but there was a tinge of relief mixed in with his grief."

Stuart's heart broke further for his brother. "Did she love him?"

"She loved Wellworth. It was always her goal. But you have not completed your explanation."

"Must I?"

"Yes, unless you wish for me to replace this in the locked drawer where I have been keeping it." He held up the journal.

Stuart contemplated snatching the book from Aaron's hands.

"Besides Miss Bennet's ability to refrain from flirting and to tolerate children, what else helped you to finally see that not all women are like Sarah?"

"She was so willing to help *me* – not just the girls – while we were on our walk and at the stream. She was put out with me for Sunday – and rightly so."

"I will not disagree with that."

Stuart had already heard his brother's thoughts on what had transpired between himself and Miss Bennet. It was not as if Stuart could hide the fact that something was not right when Aaron had arrived for dinner on Sunday as planned.

"She does not hide herself from me. She does not play games with me. She did not even seem to understand that I was about to kiss her. Sarah would have, shall we say, availed herself of my person with less provocation." She always had. Their relationship had been filled with passion – more passion than was proper for a couple who were not yet married.

"And after I stopped myself from kissing Miss Bennet – which I will have you know, would have ended very badly had I allowed my desires to satisfy themselves for I am certain she would have either slapped me or thrown me in the stream." Or more likely both.

"And you would have deserved it."

"I would have. But as I was saying. After I did not kiss her, I rose to get my and Maggie's boots and stockings so we could go for a walk, and she offered to help Maggie with hers. I turned towards her because I was once again surprised by how easily she seemed to know what I needed." He took a sip of his port. "Rose was snuggled up against her while Maggie rattled on to Rose about her boat. It was so much a picture of what I want. What I have always desired. She fits so neatly into our lives as if she were designed to be there. With Sarah, I was always trying to be what she desired."

"And the fact that Miss Bennet fits into your life and is adored by our nieces makes you think you love her?"

Stuart shook his head. "No, there was a moment when I thought she was going to cry about something. I do not even know what. But the way my heart needed to know she was well and felt like it was going to be crushed if she was not – much like it was when Maggie was angry with me on Sunday – told me I love her. And then, that tableau, which I just described, settled in my heart that I do not want a future without Miss Bennet in it." Again, he looked at Aaron and asked, "Are you certain that I have not lost my senses? Only three days ago I declared to her that I was never getting married. Never. Not to anyone."

"You have always been this way, Stu. When we were growing up, you would ponder things and once you thought you knew the right answer, you would proclaim it with the confidence of a general going into a battle he knew he would win. Many times, Broderick or I would tell you that you were wrong, but you would hold stubbornly to your views. But then, some small thing would happen, and it would be as if lightning struck you with clarity. Your point of view would shift and correct itself."

Comparing how he had felt at the moment of his realization about Miss Bennet yesterday to being struck by lightning was an excellent description. But had his point of view truly shifted to what was correct?

"Did you ever have a moment of clarity like that when courting Sarah? I know you had proposed, so I assumed you did. However, from the shocked daze that seems to be hanging around you today, I'm thinking I was wrong to assume that."

Stuart shook his head. "No, I never felt anything like this with Sarah. I thought I did when she cleverly made me believe she had agreed to marry me."

"You mean when she seduced you into helping her succeed in her scheme to be mistress of Wellworth Abbey." Aaron's voice dripped with contempt.

Stuart's eyebrows pinched together. "What do you mean she seduced me to get Wellworth?"

Aaron paged through the journal he held. "Remember how I told you that she had played brother against brother?"

"Yes."

He held out the open journal. "Maggie is your daughter."

Chapter 14

Mary placed her drawing supplies on the desk in the drawing room. She had been planning to go to the stream to do some more sketching, but she seemed unable to make herself leave the house. Memories of yesterday were still too fresh to avoid.

"Are you joining us for some sewing?" her aunt asked from where she sat near the window and next to Elizabeth on a sofa.

Mary shrugged and crossed the room to where they were. "I am not certain what I am going to do." That was true in more than one way. She had lost her heart to a gentleman who did not want her, and she had come to love his nieces as if they were her own nieces. How was she ever going to be able to bear the sorrow of being parted with them when the time came for her to leave Derbyshire?

She dropped, unceremoniously, into a comfortable chair that stood next to the sofa. Sitting here seemed as good a place as any – even if *he* had been here yesterday. Georgiana was playing the piano, or she might have gone to do that since Mr. Alford had not been in that room.

"It is not like you to wander around aimlessly," Elizabeth said. "Are you feeling well?"

Was she? It would be a relief if she were. She put a hand to her forehead. Drat! It was not any warmer than it should be. "I believe I am."

Her aunt put down the scene on which she was working. "You do not know?"

Mary sighed. "I feel strange, but I am nearly certain that I am not ill." She might be despondent, heart-sick, and melancholy, but she was not physically ill.

Her aunt's lips pursed as if she were attempting to contain a laugh. Mary saw nothing funny about the fact that she was not feeling like herself.

"Would you feel better if we were to call at Wellworth Abbey?" Aunt Gardiner shared a speaking look with Elizabeth.

"Perhaps. I do miss Maggie and Rose." She turned her attention to the view outside the window rather than looking at her aunt or sister. She knew what was being hinted at.

"Are you sure it is only Rose and Maggie whom you miss?" Elizabeth asked.

Mary lifted one shoulder and let it fall. "It does not matter."

And that was what made her feel worst of all. There was nothing that could be done to cure what ailed her, and it would get worse before there would ever be a chance of her feeling better. It was not as if Mr. Alford were going to fall at her feet and proclaim that she was the one lady who could make him reconsider his decision to never marry. She was not the sort of lady who inspired such romantic gestures. However, after yesterday's walk to the stream, she had begun to desperately wish she were.

"We will be leaving soon," her aunt's tone was full of caution.

"I know." And being reminded of that fact did nothing to help her feel any better.

"I would not wait too long before making my desires known to that young man if I were you."

"Aunt! I am not going to throw myself at a gentleman who does not want me. In fact," she added as her face began to burn, "I am not going to throw myself at any gentlemen – whether they want me or not."

Her aunt chuckled. "I am not saying that you should throw yourself at anyone, but there are ways to let him know you are interested in him and not just his nieces. You are interested in Mr. Alford, are you not?"

"I would rather not discuss it." There was no point.

"Sometimes we must do what we do not want to do."

Mary cast a sidelong glance at Aunt Gardiner, who looked just as stern as her words had sounded.

"He does not plan to marry. He told me so on Sunday."

"I know that is what he said, my dear, but that is not what his actions have shown."

Mary turned to look at her aunt.

"A gentleman who does not care would not have come to speak to your uncle and Mr. Darcy as he did."

"It was for his nieces."

"So he says, but he seemed genuinely concerned that he had offended you." One eyebrow raised over a pointed look. "And yesterday, he watched you closely when he was here."

Mary shook her head. "He was watching his nieces."

"No, he was not," Elizabeth inserted. "Even Fitzwilliam commented on it. It is the truth and not just the rapid, hopeful fancy of two ladies eager to see you happy."

"And I do not know what happened at that stream," her aunt continued, "but Mr. Alford seemed quite affected by whatever it was when he returned."

"Nothing happened." How many times was she going to have to say that there was nothing of interest to share from her walk with Mr. Alford and his nieces before Aunt Gardiner believed it? Nothing to share except that she had caught a glimpse of the future she wanted more than she had ever wanted anything before in her life.

"Something happened," her aunt assured her. "You may not have noticed it, but something most certainly happened."

"Please, can we talk about something other than wishes and hopes that can never be?"

"I would not give up on Mr. Alford just yet,"

Aunt Gardiner said. "Continue as you have been, but do not close yourself off to the possibility that you might affect him against his wishes."

Mary shook her head and rose. There was no such possibility. "I think I will go find a book to read in the library." She was not certain she would be able to focus to read, but it seemed a good way to escape this conversation.

"Mary. Look at me." Mrs. Gardiner's tone was firm, and Mary did as her aunt instructed. "You are beautiful, and I do not just mean your face, though you are by no means lacking in handsomeness. I am speaking of what is more important. Beauty that originates here." She placed a hand on her heart. "Just think about that." She picked up her embroidery. "And then, ask yourself what you would say to Maggie or Rose if either of them felt as you do."

Elizabeth pressed her lips together on a laugh when Mary gasped in surprise at their aunt's words.

Oh, it was a sneaky tactic, Mary thought as she left the room. Sneaky but effective. There was no way she would ever allow a young lady in her care to think of herself as wanting the way she allowed herself to view herself. But neither Maggie nor

Rose would be wanting. She had seen the portraits of both their mother and father. There was no way that a child born to such handsome parents would ever be lacking in beauty. Even now you could see that they would both be very pretty.

"Mary!" her uncle said as he caught her by the shoulders to keep her from running into him.

"My apologies," she said quickly. "I was not paying attention to where I was walking."

He chuckled. "I could tell you were not paying attention. However, no one was harmed, and actually, I was just coming to find you and your aunt. I am glad to see that I will not have to walk to the stream to find you. Where is your aunt?"

"She is in the drawing room with Elizabeth."

He took her hand and placed it on his arm. "I know you have likely just left my wife, since you know where she is, but I must insist that you join me in going to the drawing room. I have some news."

Mary darted a look at him. "Is it dreadful news?"

He sighed. "Not overly, but it is not happy news."

Her heart began to thump heavily. "What is it?"

"There is an issue at one of my warehouses that Mr. Waller says needs my attention."

"Mr. Waller?" She remembered the name. She had heard it somewhere.

Her uncle nodded. "A business acquaintance. I had him and Mr. Durward – they own the store that I am certain Kitty has told you about?"

Ah, yes! That was where she had heard that name before.

"I left them as contacts for my men if there should be any issues. I will assure you that what needs my attention is nothing serious, though it is of great importance. My signature is required, and the documents which need signing cannot be sent. I will have to sign them in person. Time is of the essence in this deal, so we will have to leave tomorrow."

"Tomorrow?" Her heart seemed to jump into her throat. She thought she had two weeks yet before she would have to say goodbye to Maggie and Rose – and their uncle.

"Yes. I am sorry, Mary."

"Tomorrow," she repeated. The word felt like a sentence being uttered by the magistrate, consigning her to a life of misery.

"I think it would be best if you were to call on the Alfords today," her uncle continued. "Those young ladies must not just be left with a letter of farewell."

Mary swallowed and nodded. What he said made sense, but how was she going to tell Maggie and Rose that she was leaving and not fall to pieces when doing so? They did not need a watering pot. They needed someone who could help them feel loved and secure, despite this separation that was coming before it was expected.

"I do not know if I can do that," she whispered.

Her uncle stopped just in front of the drawing room door. "You can, and you will. The Mary I know is as strong as an iron pot."

It was not an overly flattering comparison, but Mary felt the love behind the words. Uncle Gardiner believed in her abilities. That thought warmed her somewhat. However, it did not make the task before her any easier.

"I am sorry that it is necessary, but it *is* necessary," her uncle continued. "We can all go with you, or you may take just a maid or Miss Darcy."

Mary nodded. "I will take a maid." In her opinion, grieving was best done in private.

Her uncle smiled softly as if he understood just how challenging the task, which lay before her, was going to be. "I will call for the carriage. You go get yourself ready."

~*~*~

An hour and a half later, Mary stood in front of Wellworth Abbey wishing she were not an iron pot but rather a precious teacup that required coddling.

"Do you need anything else, miss?" her maid asked when Mary simply stood there on the drive next to the carriage without moving.

Someone else to do this for me, she thought. But there was no one else. So, she took a deep breath and shook her head. "No, I just need a moment to gather my thoughts." Despite the many times during the carriage ride that she had attempted to sort out the best way to tell her little friends that she was leaving, her thoughts on it were still a tangled mess.

"Very good, miss." The maid took a step backward and stood waiting until Mary finally moved forward.

"Miss Bennet, the Miss Alfords will be delighted to see you. However, their uncle is not home at present." Mr. Branston said by way of greeting when he opened the door for her to enter the house two minutes later.

"I realize this is an unexpected call," she began. "But something has happened that necessitates it."

"I trust everyone is well at Pemberley?"

"Yes, they are, but my uncle has been called back to London on business."

"Ah," the elderly gentleman said. "When do you leave us?"

"Tomorrow."

Mr. Branston smiled. "I suppose that is better than immediately."

"It is not much better." She handed her things to her maid.

"Do you remember the way to the nursery?"

Mary nodded. "I do."

"Then, shall I allow you to see yourself to it?"

"I would like that."

"Do you require me, miss?" her maid asked.

Mary shook her head. "You may rest wherever Mr. Branston says would be appropriate. Mr. Alford is not at home. I think my reputation is safe." And if her maid did not accompany her to the nursery, it meant she would not have an audience to her distress.

Slowly she climbed the family stairs, taking care to notice all the details of the woodwork of the staircase and portraits that hung on the walls. She paused on the landing that led to the library before continuing. With heavy steps, she wound her way through the corridor to the nursery.

"Miss Bennet!" Maggie cried with delight when Mary entered the room.

Despite her sadness, Mary smiled at the eager greeting. She looked around the room as she hugged first Maggie and then Rose. Was there another room in all the world where she felt so at home and as if she belonged here and only here? She brushed at the tears that such a thought brought forward.

"Are you well?" Miss Leslie asked.

"I am, but I fear I have some sad news to share." She looked at Maggie's and Rose's trusting faces. "Do you know how to post letters?"

Both heads shook in reply.

"Well, I am not entirely certain how your uncle would like you to do it, but I would imagine that you would draw whatever you wish on a piece of paper, and then, you would take it to him and ask him to send it to me. Then, when I got that letter from you, I would send you one of my own in reply. Letters are wonderful things that let people, who are far apart, talk to each other."

"You are leaving," Miss Leslie said.

Mary nodded. "My uncle has to return to London to take care of some business that only he can do. It has come as a shock to all of us, but it cannot be helped even if we wanted to help it." She knelt on the floor in front of her two little friends. "I will miss you dreadfully and will wait eagerly to hear from you."

"You are going away?" Maggie's question was barely above a whisper.

"I am. We knew it would happen eventually, did we not?" She placed a hand on Maggie's cheek. "It is just happening sooner than we expected."

Maggie threw her arms around Mary's neck. "I do not want you to leave us," she cried.

"Me either," Rose agreed as she, too, wrapped her arms as far as they would go around Mary and her sister.

"And I do not wish to leave," Mary admitted. "But I must. That is why you must know how to send me a letter. Can you draw me pictures and send them to me?"

Mary knelt on the floor wrapped in Alford misses for a long moment before Maggie gave a watery reply that they could do it.

"Will you ever come back?" she asked between sniffles.

"Whenever I can, but I do not know when that will be."

"Can you live with Miss Darcy?"

"I wish I could, sweetling. I wish I could." She squeezed both girls tight. "However, I cannot." She straightened her spine and lifted her chin, willing her emotions to stay somewhat under regulation as she dashed a tear from her cheek. "I will want to know when Rose has learned to write her name and when you have learned to read a full story by yourself. And..." She paused. There was so much she wanted to know about their lives. "You will have to tell me about how well you are learning to ride and if your uncle is successful in teaching you to swim and everything else that you are doing."

"But I cannot write all that," Maggie said.

"I will help you and so will your uncle," Miss

Leslie assured her. "Would you have time to read a story to them before you go, Miss Bennet?"

Mary nodded. "Of course. We do not leave until the morning. I think I can read a story and return home in time to not be late for that." She attempted to laugh lightly, but her success was limited. Her heart was too heavy.

After two stories in the reading chair and several more hugs later, Mary exited the nursery with a heart that ached more than it had when she had entered. She had not thought that was possible, but it most certainly seemed to be.

There was one more thing she needed to do before she took her leave of Wellworth Abbey. Miss Leslie had mentioned that the drawing room off the library was nearly finished. She simply had to peek in to see how it was going to look, and then, she would walk through the long gallery to the grand staircase before making her departure just as she had done with Mr. Alford that once.

Seeing that the drawing room was going to be just as lovely as she had imagined it would be, and then, seeing the portrait of Mr. Alford's brother did nothing to ease the ache in Mary's heart. She would miss Mr. Alford just as much, if not more, than she would miss his nieces. With any luck, he would also write her an occasional note and send it with Maggie and Rose's drawings.

She blew out a deep breath as she came to the bottom of the grand staircase.

"We will miss you," Mr. Branston said when he saw her. "You have been such a ray of hope to us all."

"Thank you. That is kind of you to say."

"And true."

Mary felt the weight of his words. She had found a place where at least a few loved her for who she was. She would tuck this feeling away and treasure it. She gathered her things from her maid and then turned to Mr. Branston.

"Would you be so kind as to make sure Mr. Alford gets this?" She held out a large envelope. "It is just a sketch that I did and that he admired. I think his nieces would enjoy it as well."

"I will gladly see that he gets it. Do take care." He held the door for her.

"I will." She stepped out into the darkest sunny day she had ever experienced to this point in her life and entered Mr. Darcy's carriage to be taken back to Pemberley before leaving all of Derbyshire and her heart behind in the morning.

Chapter 15

Stuart placed his brother's journal in the safe behind the desk in Wellworth Abbey's study where Aaron had found it shortly after Broderick's death. He would return to it on another day to read more of what his brother had written. He had read enough today to know that he was not the only one who had been injured by Sarah's actions. The knowledge did not make him miss Broderick any less, but it did help him understand why his brother had done what he did.

Sarah, he could not understand. How had she hidden such a vile nature so well? He turned the locket he held over in his hand and read the inscription – an indelible reminder of his foolishness – once again.

Forever, my love.

He opened the locket and looked at the miniature portrait it contained. Had the eyes looking back at him even known what love was back then? He shook his head. Apparently not. Or perhaps Sarah had just been that good of an actress that she could convince her audience of one – him – that what he had felt for her was love.

The door to his study opened. Quickly, Stuart snapped the locket closed and tucked it in his pocket.

"Oh! Mr. Alford!" Mr. Branston said in surprise. "We thought you were out."

"I was. I just returned a few minutes ago and slipped in here to avoid whoever was calling." He had seen a carriage on the drive and entered the house quietly through the servant's entrance because he had not wanted to see anyone. He had not even wanted his nieces to know he had returned. He had planned to make his presence known after his mind, which was a muddled mess, had cleared somewhat.

"If I had known, I would have allowed Miss Bennet to give this to you herself." His butler placed an envelope on Stuart's desk.

Miss Bennet had been here? That was her carriage? He had not expected to see her at Wellworth today. Silently, he chided himself for having shirked his duty in discovering who his caller was and missing his opportunity to see her.

"She said it was a sketch that you had admired, and she thought the Miss Alfords would also like it." Mr. Branston bowed and left the room as Stuart opened the envelope.

Inside, he found the drawing Miss Bennet had been working on near the stream when he had gone to beg her to allow Maggie and Rose to retain her friendship: one small hand rested gently in a larger one.

Attached to it was a note.

Mr. Alford,

You know this sketch is not as good as I would like it to be, but I thought it a fitting reminder of trusting even when things are imperfect.

Stuart smiled, remembering how she had apologized for the poor quality of work when she had shown him this drawing on that day. She assured him that this was precisely why she drew objects and buildings and not human forms. To him, the sketch was more than passable. In fact, he thought it was quite well-done. But then, Miss Bennet seemed to be rather severe on herself.

He turned his mind back to the rest of her missive.

I hope you will remember me fondly when you see it.

Ever your friend,

M. Bennet

Remember her fondly? His heart leapt to his throat. Anxiety and dread increased its beating. No one used those words unless they thought they would never see the other person again.

Tossing the note on his desk, he went to the study's door.

"Branston," he called.

"Yes, sir."

"Why was Miss Bennet here?" She had not said she was coming to visit the girls today. If she had, he would not have gone anywhere.

"To bid farewell to the Miss Alfords, sir."

Stuart's heart dropped to his stomach. It was as he feared. "Farewell?" he asked, hoping against hope that he had heard incorrectly.

"Yes, sir."

"As in, she is leaving Derbyshire or just not returning to visit Maggie and Rose?" Either meaning was unwelcome, but one was far worse than the other.

"Her uncle was called back to London on business."

"I see."

She was leaving Derbyshire. That was the worse option. He turned back to his study but then turned toward Branston once again. What was he supposed to do with this news? His heart felt as if it had been ripped from his chest and was about to be consigned to a pack of hungry wolves to be devoured and never returned to him.

"If it helps, sir," Branston said, "Miss Bennet and her relations do not plan to leave Pemberley until the morning."

A flicker of hope ignited within him. All might not be completely lost. "The morning, you say?"

"Yes, sir. Shall I send for your horse to be made ready?"

His butler's expression was inscrutable, but there was a hint of hopefulness in the man's voice.

Stuart shook his head and chuckled softly. "Have I truly been so obvious?" Aaron's words about recognizing Stuart's interest in Miss Bennet from their second meeting at the parsonage resounded in his mind. It seemed that it was not just Aaron who had noticed it.

"To everyone but you, sir," Branston replied.

Stuart was certain there was one other person who had not noticed his admiration for Miss Bennet, which was why he needed to be off to Pemberley at once. "I will run to the stables for my horse. There is no need to send someone else."

"Miss Bennet is a lovely young lady."

"Indeed, she is," Stuart agreed as he pulled the door to his study closed.

"She has only been gone about a quarter hour."

Stuart clapped his butler on the shoulder. "Thank you, Branston. I should be able to reach Pemberley before she does." He needed to speak to her uncle before he spoke to her. "Wish me well."

"Good luck," Branston called as Stuart raced down the hall toward the servant's entrance.

~*~*~

"Mr. Alford," Mr. Darcy said as Stuart entered the drawing room at Pemberley, "I did not expect you to call on us today."

"To be honest, I did not expect to call," Stuart admitted. He had planned to wait until tomorrow to make this particular call. "But then, this day has not gone precisely as I expected it would. Has Miss Bennet returned?"

"No, she has not."

Good. That meant he had time to gain her relations' approval before he presented his offer to her. The importance of what he was so hastily doing settled on his shoulders, weighing them down and tickling his nerves with a niggling fear of refusal.

"I heard she was at Wellworth but that I missed her." He sat down as Darcy motioned for him to do. "I was at my brother's house." He nodded a greeting to the Gardiners and Mrs. Darcy. "I also heard that you have been called back to town, Mr. Gardiner."

"I have. There are just some matters of business which cannot be done by anyone other than me. This time the thing which needs my attention is papers to sign."

"That is understandable." Not that understandable equated welcome.

"Even if it is unfortunate?" the gentleman asked as if he were reading Stuart's mind. Apparently, his wishes and desires were indeed obvious to everyone.

"Yes, even if unfortunate." Stuart rubbed his hands on his breeches. This most certainly was to be a day of unsettling conversations. He would much rather that this discussion be conducted privately with Mr. Gardiner, instead of in front of an audience of three others, but time was of the essence, and truly, what did it matter if they heard him declare his love for Miss Bennet now or later? Either way, he was going to have to face the humiliation of how wrong he had been as recently as yesterday – that day when his wrongness had started to become painfully clear to him.

"I came to a realization yesterday." He swallowed. His heart was hammering in his ears. "I was wrong." He kept his eyes on his hands, which were rubbing circles on his knees.

"About what?" Mr. Gardiner asked.

"About never wishing to marry."

"Indeed?"

There was no surprise to the question, but Stuart thought he heard a hint of laughter in it. Looking up, he noticed how poorly Mr. Gardiner was hiding his amusement. The sight brought a small amount of relief to Stuart's nerves. Amusement was a far better response than a harsh stare of disapproval, was it not?

"Yes," he answered. "It seems I need to amend my statement."

"How?"

Stuart leapt to his feet and spun towards the door to the drawing-room. Miss Bennet had some-time along the way joined them. Her eyes and nose were red, and she clutched her handkerchief tightly in one hand. He took two steps toward her. His heart cried out that he needed to comfort her, but his mind reminded him that doing so was not yet his privilege.

"I should have said that I never intend to marry anyone..." He paused and swallowed as that niggling fear of being refused once again poked at him, "unless it is you. Of course, I did not know that last part at the time, for it seems that I have been rather slow in grasping the truth of the matter."

Mrs. Darcy gave Miss Bennet a gentle shove towards Stuart. When had she risen and crossed the room? Stuart looked to the chairs in which Mr. and Mrs. Darcy and Mr. and Mrs. Gardiner had been sitting. Only Mr. Gardiner remained, and he too was standing as if ready to make a hasty departure.

"This discussion might be best conducted in private," he said with a smile. "You have my blessing *if* you can secure hers." He nodded to Miss Bennet.

"I do?"

Mr. Gardiner nodded. "We can discuss particulars about your suitableness later, but our Mary is a sensible lady. I know she would not be taken in by a scoundrel. I also know that scoundrels do not go out of their way to care for children as you do your nieces. I wish you well." And with that, he also left the room.

Stuart turned back to Miss Bennet, the only other occupant of the room and the most important person in Stuart's world at present.

"You wish to marry me?" she asked. He could hear the disbelief in her voice.

"Yes."

"But on Sunday, you said –"

"I love you," he interjected. "I did not know that on Sunday. I only discovered it yesterday, and honestly, I would not present you with an offer so soon after so recently coming to understand that fact myself. However, you are leaving tomorrow, and I cannot, will not, let you go without telling you that I intend to court you until you are convinced that I am worthy of you." He took her by the elbow and led her to the sofa on which the Darcys had been sitting for she looked as if she might faint.

She shook her head as she sat down. "Gentlemen like you do not marry ladies like me."

"We do if they will accept us," he replied with a slightly teasing grin as he knelt before her and took her hand. "I believe we already discussed that. I am not the sort of gentleman who wishes to marry a pretty accessory. I am the sort of gentleman who wants a delightfully rare and precious lady as his wife."

She looked at him warily, but at least, she did not try to argue with him about how he saw her. He hoped that was because she wanted him for a husband.

"This all seems a bit sudden."

"It is sudden. However, when I discussed it with Aaron today, he assured me that this is how I am when it comes to making discoveries."

"You discussed me with your brother?" Her eyes were wide.

"Yes. I thought I might be losing my senses."

One eyebrow arched in an accusing fashion.

"Because it was so sudden," he said quickly. "It was not because I thought that loving you was only possible if I lost my senses. I just was..." He sat back on his heels. This was Miss Bennet. To her, he could speak frankly. He did not need to pretend to understand all that was occurring between them.

"How does one fall in love in an instant?" he asked with a shake of his head. "Not that it was in an instant, I suppose, but it felt as if it was. One moment I was happy to be your friend and then, the next, I knew I would never be happy again if you were not always by my side as my wife."

He released his grip on her hand to run his hand through his hair. "Aaron assures me that I am still in possession of my sense. I know it does not sound as if I am." He rose from the floor and plopped himself on the sofa next to her. He was doing an extremely poor job of explaining himself to her, though she did not look put off by it at all. Oh, how he loved her!

"It has been a trying day. My mind is not as ordered as it should be," he admitted. "I tried to put my thoughts in order while riding here, but as you can tell, it did not happen."

She angled herself to look at him. "What made your day so trying?"

Of course, she would inquire after his troubles

rather than pressing for him to explain himself more thoroughly, and he knew why she did it. Miss Bennet possessed a heart that was as gracious as her ways of thinking were odd.

"It is a bit difficult to explain." How was he supposed to tell her about Sarah? It was not a question of *should* he tell her. He knew he must. Miss Bennet did not prevaricate, and if she found out about Maggie later? Well, he had already caught a glimpse of her temper on Sunday, and he was certain he did not wish to feel her full wrath.

He pulled the locket from his pocket. "Aaron gave me Broderick's journal and this locket." He took her hand and placed the necklace in it. "Broderick took this from his wife before she could give it to Maggie."

"Why would he do that? It is beautiful." She smiled at the words on the back of it before she opened it.

"That locket was a gift to Sarah from Maggie's father, which she intended to tell Maggie."

"I still do not understand why your brother would not allow his wife to give Maggie such a special gift. I would like it excessively if my mother gave me something that had originally been a token of my father's love for her." She was looking closely at the painting, so Stuart simply waited until the truth became apparent.

"This portrait is very well done. It looks just like the one in the long galler—" Wide, questioning eyes rose to his.

"You noticed the nose?"

She nodded.

"It is me."

Her eyes widened further in shock and was that horror? How was he ever going to convince her to marry him once she heard this twisted tale?

"I am Maggie's father, although, until today, I did not know that."

Once again, she looked as if she was going to faint.

"Sarah and I were betrothed, or I thought we were, though as I have been thinking about it today, I have realized that she never said she was going to marry me. She always just said she was going to soon be a married woman, and, therefore, indiscretions did not frighten her."

Miss Bennet slumped backwards on the sofa. "You and she...?"

He nodded. "And Maggie is the result."

"Why are you telling me this?"

"Because I love you, and I would never lie to you. Never. You do not prevaricate, and neither will I." He took the locket from her and put it back in his pocket.

"Will you tell Maggie?"

"I do not know. She has a father – Broderick. I do not want to take his place in her heart, and I would not want to do anything to destroy the memories she has of him or her mother."

She placed her hand over his where it rested on his leg. It was a small gesture but one which he hoped was filled with a little bit of the acceptance and forgiveness he sought.

"How did your brother end up being Maggie's father?" she asked gently. There was no censure, no condemnation in her tone. "I know I likely should not ask, but..."

"No," he assured her. "I want you to know." He needed her to know.

He turned his hand over under hers and laced his finger with hers. "A month after I had left for Devon to take up my new position, my brother woke to find Sarah in his bed. He had partaken of far more alcohol than he should have the night before and thought that he had seduced her while foxed."

"Oh, my." The comment was barely above a whisper.

"Tell me if what I am saying is too much for you."

She nodded.

"As it turns out, she had staged the entire scene, knowing that she was already pregnant with my child." Disgust filled him now as it had earlier today when Sarah's scheme had been laid open before him.

"Why would she do that?" Agony seemed to drip from Miss Bennet's words.

"Some people love money and position far more than they should." That was all Sarah had truly ever loved – money and position, not him, not Broderick, and perhaps not even Maggie and Rose.

"Broderick was the heir to Wellworth," he continued. "I was not. Broderick would have never courted her because he knew I liked her." He blew out a breath. "That was why I felt so betrayed by Broderick, I thought he had stolen Sarah from me. I did not know that Sarah had stolen him from me." He fell silent, and Miss Bennet waited patiently for him to continue.

"Sarah went to Broderick claiming to be pregnant with his child, and he did what he thought he had to do. He married her. He did not even suspect that the child might not be his. He knew nothing of Sarah's scheme until he saw her with that necklace, which was just after Rose was born. I knew nothing about her scheme until Aaron let me read it in Broderick's journal today."

Miss Bennet remained silent but her grip on his hand tightened. He could feel her compassion flowing through the points where their skin touched.

"I never loved her. I thought I did. I honestly thought I did." He shook his head. "But it was not an abiding love. I just did not understand that until I met you and your family. Please, do not ask me to explain that. I am not entirely certain that I can."

Silence settled between them but not uncomfortably so.

"If you thought you loved her but were wrong, how do you know you are not wrong now? Perhaps you think you love me because Maggie and Rose do."

He lifted her hand to his lips. "I will not lie. I love the way you care for them and they, for you.

However, my telling you that I love you and wish to marry you is purely selfish. You are my other half, and it is not my head that has told me that. It is my heart. Indeed, my head has only just figured out what my heart has been telling me since your first visit to Wellworth."

He untangled his fingers from hers and then, carefully arranged her hand in his to look like the drawing she had given him. "Does it look right?" he asked.

"How is it supposed to look?" Her brow was furrowed in confusion.

"Like your drawing."

Her brow smoothed and her lips curled into a sweet smile. "It does."

"Will you trust me with your hand even if I am so deplorably imperfect? If you do, I promise you that I will protect you from all that I can, but I cannot promise to be able to protect you from every ill. There just is no protection from some things. Even if I wish there were." His eyes fixed on hers.

She nodded. "I will."

He cupped her face in his hands. "And I will trust you with mine." He smiled. "Even if you, too, are imperfect."

She gasped, but he prevented her from speaking by pressing his lips to hers.

"I love you, but no one is perfect, Miss Bennet," he said after he had broken their quick kiss. "However, I do think you are pretty close to perfection."

"I am not—"

He cut off her protest with another kiss. This time it was one that was much longer and was only broken when someone, somewhere behind Stuart, cleared his throat.

"I take it you have her blessing?" Mr. Gardiner asked.

"Surprisingly, yes," Stuart answered. He rose from the sofa and pulled Miss Bennet up with him.

"And when will the happy day be?" her uncle asked.

"That, we have not discussed. There was far too much to discuss about my stupidity." He smiled at Mary who had gasped softly at his comment. "However, I am thinking sometime in the autumn. That will give us some time to get to know one another better through letters. Would that be acceptable to you, Miss Bennet?"

"I think you can call her Mary now," Mr. Gardiner offered. "Can he not, my dear?"

"Yes, and yes."

"And you may call me Stuart," he replied. Sarah had never given him permission to use her name, nor had she waited to gain his permission to use his. It was just another way in which Mary outshone her. How had he ever thought that Sarah had been a prize worth chasing?

"Do you know how wonderful you are?" he asked.

"No." Her brow was furrowed, and her expression said she thought he may have lost his mind. He truly loved how she lacked any trace of arrogance about her person.

"Sadly, she does not," her uncle agreed. "But I do think that you, sir, are just the gentleman to help her learn what many of us have always known." He placed a hand on Stuart's shoulder. "Now, if you have a few minutes before you head back to Wellworth, I would like to go over what you have to offer our Mary besides your affection and the good sense to see her value."

He looked at Mary and then back at Stuart. "Darcy's study is the second door on the right. I will expect you to be there in five minutes, and

I will expect my wife and Elizabeth to be here in four. Use your time wisely."

Stuart waited until Mr. Gardiner had exited the room. Then, he drew Mary into his embrace. "I am going to go home and tell Maggie and Rose that they will have a new aunt in the autumn."

"You are certain that you are not marrying me for them?"

"No," he replied with a laugh. "They are benefiting from my very selfish decision." He lowered his lips to hers. "I love you, Mary."

"And I love you," she whispered just before he claimed her lips in a kiss that stirred a fire deep within his soul, a fire that had never before been touched. It was both thrilling and a trifle unsettling, if he were to be honest, but then, this had been a day of unsettling events.

Chapter 16

[*Two Months Later*]

Mary sat up straighter and looked expectantly at the tray Mr. Hill brought into the sitting room at Longbourn.

"There is nothing here for you, my dear," her father said with a chuckle. "I dare say I never thought I would see the day that my Mary would be as eager for the mail to arrive as her mother and younger sisters are."

Honestly, Mary had never thought such a day would come either. Just like she had never thought she would find a gentleman like Stuart who would love her as he did.

Her father rose and handed an envelope to Kitty. "It appears to be from Mrs. Crawford, though I would be completely astonished if it did not contain news about her brother. I suppose this will be the last letter I get to deliver to you." He kissed the top of her head. "I will miss it."

He straightened. "Who will keep your mother entertained when you are all gone?"

"Papa," Kitty scolded softly.

"There is still Lydia," Mary said.

"But only until next summer," Lydia protested. "Then, I shall go to the sea with Uncle Gardiner as he has promised, and there, I will find a husband." She pursed her lips. "That is, of course, if I do not find one here first. I heard that Mrs. Andrew's nephew is coming for a visit in November."

"Mrs. Andrew's nephew?" Mrs. Bennet cried with delight. "Oh, I remember him as being quite the attractive young fellow. How long has it been since we saw him?" she asked Mr. Bennet.

"I could not rightly tell you, my dear. I do not make it a practice to keep a calendar of the comings and goings of every handsome gentleman who enters the neighborhood."

"I believe it was six years ago," Kitty inserted. "I remember we were not allowed to attend the soiree at Mrs. Andrew's house but Jane was. She told us all about him."

Lydia sighed. "I do hope he is just as handsome now as he was then."

"As do I," her mother agreed.

Mary shook her head. The two of them, Lydia and Mama, had always been so much alike. A gentleman's handsomeness, fortune, and dancing ability were paramount in determining how marriageable he was.

She smiled to herself as she added a smudge of shading to her drawing. She had always hoped to marry someone who was somewhat handsome and in possession of a comfortable fortune. However, those had never been the most important things to her. A gentleman's character had been highest on her list. Happily, she had found a gentleman who possessed all of those things – handsomeness, fortune, and good character.

She sighed. If only there had been a letter in the mail. As of today, it had been two weeks since Mr. Alford's last letter.

"I think I am going to go for a walk," she said as she tucked her sketch away.

"May I come with you?" Kitty asked.

"Are you not occupied with your letter?"

She shook her head. "Not presently. I think I would prefer to read it near the rose garden."

"Lydia will still look over your shoulder," Mary muttered.

Kitty chuckled. "Perhaps, but Mama will not," she whispered.

"Oh, there is someone here!" Lydia cried from her seat at the window that faced the drive. "It is a most elegant conveyance," she said to her mother. "I wonder who it can be?"

Mrs. Bennet wasted no time in joining Lydia at the window. An unfamiliar carriage was no matter to brush aside for a lady like her who loved company more than anything.

"I do not know who that is," she said. "I am certain I have never seen that carriage before. Kitty, does it belong to Mr. Linton or perhaps one of his friends?"

"Why would Mr. Linton's friends be calling on us? The wedding is not for five more days," Kitty replied, as she peeked out the window.

"Jane said she was expecting guests to arrive a few days early."

"Which guests?" Mary crowded into the bay window with her sisters and mother.

"She did not say," Mrs. Bennet replied. "I wonder who it could be."

"Oh!" Mary cried before dashing toward the door. He was here!

"Do you know who it is?" her mother called after her.

Mr. Bennet chuckled as he checked his pocket watch. "It appears Mary's young man is punctual."

His words caught Mary's attention before she could duck out of the room. "You knew Mr. Alford was coming?"

Her father nodded and made a shooing motion. "It is best if you greet him before your mother does."

She did not have to be told that twice. She most certainly wanted to greet Stuart before her mother did.

"Mary!" Maggie's delighted cry greeted her as she hurried out the front door and down the steps.

"Mary!" Rose joined her sister in expressing her pleasure as her uncle lifted her from the carriage.

Turning, Stuart added his own, "Mary!"

She shook her head. They were a silly trio, but she could not and would not fault them for making her feel so special as they did with their greeting.

"I did not know you were coming," she said as she knelt to give the girls a hug.

"It was a seqwet," Rose whispered.

"You kept it very well," Mary said, looking up at Stuart who looked positively pleased with himself.

"Uncle Stuart has a surprise for you," Maggie whispered.

"Does he?"

She nodded. "It is for later." She cast a wary look in her uncle's direction. "I cannot tell you what it is."

"And I will not ask you." Mary squeezed her tight. "I am so happy to see you. I have missed you both."

"And me?" Stuart asked.

"Yes, and you," Mary said as she stood. She would love to give him a hug as she had his nieces, but they were in the front of the house and her mother and sisters were approaching.

"Oh, my, he is handsome," she heard her mother say and cringed.

She glanced over her shoulder. It was as expected, her father was the only sensible Bennet to remain in the sitting room and wait for introductions to be made. "Mr. Alford, may I introduce you and your nieces to my mother and sisters?"

"We would be delighted to make their acquaintance," he replied just as Mrs. Bennet, Lydia, and Kitty joined them.

"Mama, Kitty, and Lydia, this is Mr. Stuart Alford, Miss Maggie Alford, and Miss Rose Alford. Stuart, Maggie, and Rose, this is my mother and two of my sisters, Kitty and Lydia."

"And Miss Kitty is the one getting married, am I correct?" Stuart asked.

"Yes," Maggie answered.

Kitty smiled. "Yes, I am the one getting married."

"She is my third daughter to marry." Mrs. Bennet said proudly.

"Fourth to marry," Kitty corrected.

Mrs. Bennet blinked. "No, third. First was Jane. Second was Lizzy. Third is you."

Kitty shook her head. "Third is Mary." Her eyes danced with excitement. "I just heard the news from Mr. Linton. He asked his sister to include it in her letter."

Mary looked from Kitty to her mother and then to Stuart. "I do not understand. Is Mr. Linton postponing the wedding?"

Maggie pulled her hand, drawing her attention. "It is a surprise," she whispered when Mary looked down at her.

"It is a seqwet," Rose agreed while nodding her head.

"The girls and I have been in town seeing to some business." Stuart looked a trifle uneasy. "It seemed best to get it done before arriving for your sister's wedding. While we were in town, Maggie said she did not want to go home without you."

"You did?" Mary asked Maggie, who nodded.

"And Rose and I agreed that we did not want to go home without you either. So, I sought out Mr. Linton and he agreed to allow us to marry directly before him. That is, he agreed to it so long as it was acceptable to Miss Kitty."

"You did?" Her eyes shifted from him to Kitty. His words from his letters that said he was eager to have her as his wife most certainly were not merely pretty words, but then, she had not really expected them to be. Stuart was nothing if not honest and direct with her. Still, she was amazed that he had acted on those words.

"And I am happy to allow you to marry before me," Kitty said.

"You are?" Lydia said with no little amount of surprise. "I would not want to give away my precedence."

"And that is why you are still too young to marry," Kitty retorted.

"I am only fifteen months younger than you," Lydia grumbled.

"What exactly do you mean by *directly before*?" Mrs. Bennet asked.

"That is up to Mary, Miss Kitty, and of course, yourself, ma'am."

"Discussions are much easier to enjoy over a cup of tea when conducted in the house, my dear," Mr. Bennet called from the doorway.

"Oh, yes! Do come in Mr. Alford." She crouched down. "It is a pleasure to meet you, Miss Alford and Miss Rose."

The two girls dipped a curtsey.

"Do you like tea?" Mrs. Bennet asked.

"Very much!" Maggie said.

"Yes, please," Rose added as she slipped her hand into Mary's while Maggie took Mrs. Bennet's proffered one.

Mary moved to follow her mother and sisters, but Stuart pulled her back.

249

"You do not care if I kiss Mary, do you, Rose?" he asked.

She shook her head and closed her eyes.

"What have you been teaching them?" Mary teased after he had given her a half embrace and a quick kiss – much too quick. She would not admit it to just anyone, but she had been dreaming about kissing him again every night, and often during the day, since she had left Pemberley.

"Miss Leslie will be shocked," he agreed with a laugh. "However, she will have to adjust to my belief that children should not wonder whether or not their parents – or aunt and uncle, in this case – love each other. Kisses and hugs between *a husband and wife*," he shot a look at Rose, who nodded, "are perfectly acceptable."

Mary considered pointing out to him that they were not yet husband and wife, but there was no way she was going to present him with a reason to not kiss her. She liked it far too much. Her cheeks grew warm at the thought.

"Mr. Alford," Mr. Bennet greeted as they walked in the door, "it seems I will have to let you marry my daughter after that display." He chuckled as he shook Stuart's hand. "I never thought it would be

Mary who would find a gentleman so willing to thwart propriety."

"We were not thwarting propriety," Mary protested weakly, despite knowing that it was not common practice for ladies to kiss gentlemen while standing on the drive.

Her father winked at her. "I believe I can overlook it this once." He looked down at Rose. "And who is this lovely little lady?"

"This is Rose," Stuart replied.

"And Maggie is your sister?"

"Yes," Rose answered.

"Shall we go plan a wedding?" he asked her.

A smile lit her little face. "Yes, please."

He held his hand out to her.

She looked up at Mary.

"Go ahead," she encouraged. "He is a very good Papa."

"One more," Mr. Bennet said to Stuart as Rose took his hand. "But if you do not hurry, your wedding will be decided for you."

"I have missed you," Stuart said once Mr. Bennet had left them alone in the hall.

"Not nearly as much as I have missed you. There

was only one of me to miss, and I had three of you to miss."

He chuckled. "Do you know how wonderful you are?"

He had been telling her in each and every one of his letters just how wonderful he thought she was and had always ended his comments with "and I will entertain no arguments of my being wrong on the subject, though I suspect I will hear a few anyway." And he had heard a few, much to his delight he had assured her.

"I am beginning to," she replied before he pulled her into his arms and kissed her as thoroughly as he had that day, many weeks ago, in the drawing room at Pemberley. And while it was not a short kiss, it was still too quick for Mary.

However, it would not be long until her opportunities to kiss Stuart would be far less limited. It would only be five days to be exact.

Mr. Aaron Alford arrived at Netherfield the same day that Mr. and Mrs. Henry Crawford, Mr. Linton, and his Aunt Gwladys did, and the following day, Mary and Stuart, along with Kitty and Mr. Linton, stood at the front of Longbourn's church, pledging themselves to each other.

Maggie and Rose sat between their uncle and their new Grandmama, which was the name Mrs. Bennet insisted upon being called. Mary feared her mother would be the ruin of the two youngsters for Lydia had been displaced. Mrs. Bennet had found two new young ladies to spoil, and Mary was happy that their stay in Hertfordshire would not be so long that any real damage could be done.

Lydia seemed to bear her displacement well, but then, that was likely because Mr. Aaron Alford was both handsome and unmarried. It did not matter to Lydia that he seemed to pay more attention to Georgiana than her. She was just content to have someone at whom she could bat her eyes.

Mary was happy to allow her to do so, for she was far too busy stepping into her wonderful future to be worried about her little sister.

And Stuart? Well, a week later, as he arrived at Wellworth Abbey, he knew beyond a shadow of a doubt that no matter the season, Derbyshire was indeed the most beautiful place in the world, for it was where he had found true, abiding love in the eyes of two young girls and the heart of his lovely wife.

Theirs would be a happy home. While its halls

would often ring with the sounds of children's laughter and its walls – particularly those in the small drawing room between the library and music room – would proudly display Mary's sketches, deep in the quiet corners and private rooms, whispers of secrets from times gone by and hopes for the future would be shared between husband and wife. Just as they had been during their very first summer.

Before You Go

If you enjoyed this book, be sure to let others
know by leaving a review.

~*~*~

Want to know when other books in this series
will be available?
You can always know what's new with my
books by subscribing to my mailing list.
(There will, of course, be a thank you gift for
joining because I think my readers are awesome!)
Book News from Leenie Brown
(bit.ly/LeenieBBookNews)

~*~*~

Turn the page to read an excerpt from another
one of Leenie's books.

Marrying Elizabeth Excerpt

[If you like Pride and Prejudice variation series, such as the Darcy Family Holidays series, that begin with a departure from canon in book one that expands out into a new Austen-inspired world in the following books, you might enjoy the Marrying Elizabeth series. Below is chapter one from book one, Confounding Caroline.]

CHAPTER 1

Fitzwilliam Darcy handed his coat and beaver to his friend's butler, while that friend, Charles Bingley, leaned nonchalantly against the sitting room's door frame. The soft glow of a lamp, which remained lit, shone behind him, indicating that Bingley had been engaged in some activity in the room before which he now stood.

"I had hoped you would be home, but I did not

expect it," Darcy said in greeting. It was not Bingley's normal wont to remain at home. "Reading?" he queried with some surprise as he took note of the book in Bingley's hand.

Bingley shrugged. "I do read on occasion."

"I would not wish to keep you from your amusements." Darcy smirked slightly. If he knew his friend, Bingley would likely not mind the disruption since Bingley preferred people to books.

Bingley shook his head and chuckled. "Come, my study would be more comfortable than the sitting room and less likely to be invaded by females should Caroline return early."

"I am surprised you did not accompany her to the Grahams' soiree," Darcy said as he followed Bingley into the study.

"I have had my fill of ferrying Caroline around only to have her turn up her pert little nose at every gentleman she meets, so I sent her with Louisa and Hurst."

He tucked his book away on a shelf behind his desk, and then opening the door on the right side of his desk, he pulled out a bottle of amber coloured liquid and two glasses.

"I find I tire of society. It is always the same.

The same ladies in different dresses with different coloured hair and hats, but the same gossip, the same weather, the same pleasantries. It's just so much of the same, over and over and over and over." He handed a glass to Darcy and smiled. "Besides, if I am not mistaken, I will not be the only one who will enjoy this Caroline-free evening."

Darcy chuckled "The quiet is agreeable to me, but you have never enjoyed silence so much as I." There was something different about Bingley the past few weeks. He did not smile as much as was his usual wont, and he seemed to tuck himself away in his study more and more. Darcy swirled the liquid in his glass and threw one leg over the other. The leather squeaked as he shifted in the chair across from Bingley.

Bingley sighed. "I find I am longing for the country, but Caroline will hear nothing of leaving town when there are so many functions to attend." He took a draught from his glass. "If I thought she meant to find a husband, trotting her around to the various venues might not be so bothersome, but she is not intent on snaring anyone but you."

Darcy knew that fact very well. Caroline had never been reserved in demonstrating her preference for him over every gentleman she met. "A title and a larger fortune might dissuade her."

The hint of bitterness in Bingley's laugh surprised Darcy almost as much as Bingley's wishing to leave town and avoid society. These were not Bingley actions. They were behaviours that were more likely to be attributed to Darcy rather than his gregarious friend.

"She is as stubborn as a mule," Bingley muttered, "and almost as bright."

Darcy's brows rose. He was not surprised by the fact that Bingley was complaining about his sister. He had heard Bingley complain about Caroline before — many times. However, he had never heard Bingley complain about anything more than her incessant need to purchase fripperies and dresses or the way she nattered on about this person or that. There was something decidedly wrong with his friend, and Darcy had a sinking feeling that he knew just what it was.

"You surprise me," Darcy said, not wishing to broach the topic of the cause of the change in Bingley but knowing it was necessary. "Was it not you who claimed to be happy wherever you were, be it town or country?"

"That was before," Bingley said over the rim of his glass.

"Before what?" Darcy prodded.

"Before I took an estate." Bingley shifted in his chair uneasily, studying the painting above the fireplace for a few moments before allowing his attention to return to his friend. He sighed deeply as his gaze fell to where Darcy's foot slowly bounced up and down.

Surreptitiously, Darcy glanced at his friend. He recognized Bingley's sigh, for it was the same groan of uncertainty that had taken up residence in his own chest. It was a new and unwelcome feeling, and it was not something that, though he had tried, he could command away. He had not been able to erase it with busyness, nor had he been able to wash it away with drink. There remained only one option for dealing with such uncertainty and its pretty reason. It must be acknowledged for what it was. The root of it must be exposed, then left to wither away with time — at least, for him. For his friend, he hoped for a different outcome.

"Is it the estate or the society in Hertfordshire that you miss, my friend?" Darcy's voice was quiet, and he fixed his eyes on the wall beyond Bingley's head. A small smile played at his mouth as he contemplated the image of smiling eyes and an impertinent grin that always came to his mind when he thought of Hertfordshire. "Netherfield seems like a fine estate, and the neighbourhood was not without its enchantments." He sipped his drink and then swirled it again, watching the liquid swirl up the sides of the glass.

"I thought you loathed the inhabitants of Hertfordshire." Bingley's voice was filled with incredulity. "Is that not why you and my sisters were so hasty in joining me in town — the people are beneath us, there is no society worth keeping, that sort of thing?

Again, Darcy's brows rose at the rancor in Bingley's voice. He sighed heavily, and colour crept up his cheeks. This would not be a pleasant discussion.

"I did not loathe all of the inhabitants. I found some of them to be quite delightful — so delightful, in fact, that leaving seemed safer than staying." He rose and walked to the window. Admitting his folly and weakness would be easier if he were able to move about and not have to face the friend whom he had, he suspected, unknowingly injured.

Bingley drummed his fingers on the arm of his chair and raised a brow in anticipation of an expected explanation.

"She is here in town." Darcy placed his empty glass on a side table and allowed his eyes to remain on it rather than look at his friend.

"Who is here in town?"

Darcy drew a deep breath and spared Bingley only a glance before returning his gaze to his glass. "Miss Bennet."

"Miss Bennet?"

Darcy nodded.

"How do you know?" Bingley was on his feet and pacing. "Have you seen her?"

Darcy shook his head and sighed. "No, I have not seen her, but your sisters have." He turned once again toward the window. Bingley's reaction to the news was as expected and proved to Darcy how deeply attached his friend was to Miss Bennet.

"My sisters?" Bingley stood beside his friend, his brows drawn together in question.

Darcy turned toward him. "This afternoon, while you were out, I came by to drop off those papers." He pointed to the packet sitting unopened on the somewhat cluttered desk. "Caroline informed me that Miss Bennet had called."

"She was here? Miss Bennet was here?" Bingley's eyes were wide with astonishment. "Why did Caroline not tell me?"

Darcy wished to walk away from his friend, so that he could not see the pain in Bingley's eyes, but he would not. "It seems your sister is actively trying to separate you and Miss Bennet. She seemed to think I would be impressed by her belittling of the inferior society of the country." He paused and drew a deliberate breath. "At one time I would have agreed with her, but I no longer do."

Bingley crossed his arms and studied his friend.

Darcy winced under the examination, but it was not more than he deserved. Unable to bear both his shame and the scrutiny of his friend any longer, he turned back to the window. "I have to make a confession, Bingley. You may wish to throw me out of your home when I am finished, and I will fully understand if you do." Darcy continued to stare out the window, but he could feel the eyes of his friend boring into him.

"I wished to separate you from Miss Bennet when we left Hertfordshire." He closed his eyes as he heard his friend's muttered oath. "I told you she seemed indifferent to you. While it is true that I did not notice any particular regard for you on her part, it is not the reason I wished to separate you from her. It is not even the connection to her family or the supposed inferior society of Meryton that led me to take the actions I did." He swallowed and drew a deep fortifying breath before continuing. "I did not wish for you to become attached to Miss Bennet, for it would place me in an awkward situation. I was being completely and utterly selfish." He turned to look at his friend. "I am sorry," he whispered.

"An awkward situation?" Bingley wore a look of displeasure Darcy had rarely seen. "You would separate me from the woman I loved because it would somehow make your life awkward?"

Darcy nodded slowly. "Yes."

"Explain yourself," Bingley demanded, "for I do not have the pleasure of understanding your meaning."

Darcy shrugged one shoulder. "I thought if we left, if you and Miss Bennet were not allowed to become attached, I could avoid the danger, but I have discovered that the danger is not confined to

Hertfordshire. It has followed me here to town. It haunts me day and night." He turned back towards the window as he continued.

"I am expected to marry well, to make a match that will increase the wealth and position of my family. It is what my father and uncle have always taught me."

"You are still making no sense."

Darcy could hear the exasperation in his friend's voice. It was rather how he had felt since leaving Hertfordshire — annoyed, disturbed, and vexed by the memory of Miss Elizabeth Bennet.

"How would my being fortunate enough to marry a lady such as Miss Bennet," Bingley continued, "impose upon some imagined need of yours to marry a lady of wealth and standing?"

"Miss Bennet has sisters," Darcy said to the darkness of the night before him.

"Yes, four," Bingley retorted. "I still do not see —"

"But only one," Darcy interrupted, "with the musical laughter of a brook, eyes as expressive as any the masters have painted, and a mind that is..." he shook his head "so quick, so very quick and keen."

Darcy blew out a breath. "I imagined one day I would find a woman who would meet all the qualifications my uncle and father had taught me are necessary for the wife of a man of my standing and that we would eventually learn to esteem one another. But, I cannot fathom such a match after..." His voice trailed off.

A hand grasped his shoulder. "After meeting the one person you find you do not wish to live without." It was not a question that Bingley asked but rather a statement of deep understanding.

Darcy gave his friend a sad smile and nodded mutely.

"Now, you know why I am longing for the country," Bingley said softly.

Darcy nodded again. "I suspected as much. It is why I came here tonight — to discover if I was correct. I will not stand in your way. You deserve happiness. You have been a good friend to me, and I would not want to part for any other reason." Darcy turned to leave.

"What do you mean part?" Bingley asked. "I do not hate you for what you have done if that is what has you worried. I am not happy, but I am not angry. There is no reason for us to part."

Darcy stood with his hand on the doorknob. "I do not think I can bear hearing of her, especially when she belongs to another. It is just too much." His shoulders slumped. "You shall always remain my friend, Bingley. I will always be ready to serve you in any way, but please...please, do not ask me to be a witness to that."

Acknowledgements

There are many who have had a part in the creation of this story. Some have read and commented on it. Some have proofread for grammatical errors and plot holes. Others have not even read the story and a few, I know, will never read it. However, their encouragement and belief in my ability, as well as their patience when I became cranky or when supper was late or the groceries ran low, was invaluable.

First and foremost, I want to thank God for giving me the passion, ability, and opportunity to write. Then, I would also like to say *thank you* to Zoe, Rose, Kristine, Ben, and Kyle, as well as my Patreon patrons, who followed this story as it developed and waited, as patiently as one might do, from one Friday to the next, to read a new chapter. I feel blessed through your help, support, and understanding.

Next, I would like to extend a special thank you to Leslie E. for submitting an estate name option when I asked for help in the Sigh-worthy Romance Tearoom Facebook group. Wellworth Abbey and Miss Leslie have their names because of your willingness to help me out with that.

And finally, I want to thank my husband for, without his somewhat pushy insistence that I start sharing my writing, none of my writing goals and dreams would have been met. I love you dearly.

More Books by Leenie

You can find all of Leenie's books at this link
bit.ly/LeenieBBooks
where you can explore the collections below

~*~

Other Pens, Mansfield Park

~*~

Touches of Austen

~*~

Dash of Darcy and Companions Collection

~*~

Marrying Elizabeth Series

~*~

Sweet Possibilities, A Darcy and Elizabeth Variations Collection

~*~

Willow Hall Romances

~*~

The Choices Series

~*~

Darcy Family Holidays

~*~

Darcy and... An Austen-Inspired Collection

~*~

Nature's Fury and Delights (A Sweet Regency Novelettes Series)

About the Author

Leenie Brown has always been a girl with an active imagination, which, while growing up, was both an asset, providing many hours of fun as she played out stories, and a liability, when her older sister and aunt would tell her frightening tales. At one time, they had her convinced Dracula lived in the trunk at the end of the bed she slept in when visiting her grandparents!

Although it has been years since she cowered in her bed in her grandparents' basement, she still has an imagination which occasionally runs away with her, and she feeds it now as she did then — by reading!

Her heroes, when growing up, were authors, and the worlds they painted with words were (and still are) her favourite playgrounds! Now, as an adult, she spends much of her time in the Regency world, playing with the characters from her favourite Jane Austen novels and those of her own creation.

When she is not traipsing down a trail in an attempt to keep up with her imagination, Leenie resides in the beautiful province of Nova Scotia with her two sons and her very own Mr. Brown (a wonderful mix of all the best of Darcy, Bingley, and Edmund with a healthy dose of the teasing Mr. Tilney and just a dash of the scolding Mr. Knightley).

Connect with Leenie

E-mail:

LeenieBrownAuthor@gmail.com

Facebook:

www.facebook.com/LeenieBrownAuthor

Blog:

leeniebrown.com

Patreon:

https://www.patreon.com/LeenieBrown

Subscribe to Leenie's Mailing List:

Book News from Leenie Brown

(bit.ly/LeenieBBookNews)

Made in the USA
Monee, IL
04 September 2021

77384155R00154